VAMPIRE HUNTER D

Other Vampire Hunter D books published by
Dark Horse Books and Digital Manga Publishing

VAMPIRE HUNTER D

VOLUME 15

DARK ROAD

PART THREE

Written by

HIDEYUKI KIKUCHI

Illustrations by

YOSHITAKA AMANO

English translation by

KEVIN LEAHY

Dark Horse Books®   Digital Manga Publishing

Milwaukie   Los Angeles

VAMPIRE HUNTER D 15: DARK ROAD
PART THREE
© Hideyuki Kikuchi, 1999. Originally published in Japan in 1999 by ASAHI SONORAMA Co.
English translation copyright © 2010 by Dark Horse Books and Digital Manga Publishing.

Cover art by Yoshitaka Amano
English translation by Kevin Leahy
Book design by Krystal Hennes

Published by
Dark Horse Books
A division of Dark Horse Comics, Inc.
10956 SE Main Street
Milwaukie, OR 97222
darkhorse.com

Digital Manga Publishing
1487 West 178th Street, Suite 300
Gardena, CA 90248
dmpbooks.com

Library of Congress Cataloging-in-Publication Data

Kikuchi, Hideyuki, 1949-
 [D--Daku rodo. English]
 Dark road. Part Three / written by Hideyuki Kikuchi ; illustrated by Yoshitaka Amano; English translation by Kevin Leahy. -- 1st Dark Horse Books ed.
    p. cm. -- (Vampire Hunter D ; v. 15)
 "Originally published in Japan in 1999 by ASAHI"--T.p. verso.
 ISBN 978-1-59582-500-1
 I. Amano, Yoshitaka. II. Leahy, Kevin. III. Title.
 PL832.I37D2513 2010
 895.6'36--dc22
                                    2010018183

First Dark Horse Books Edition: August 2010
10 9 8 7 6 5 4 3 2 1
Printed at Lake Book Manufacturing, Inc., Melrose Park, IL, USA

VAMPIRE HUNTER D

Dark Road

PART THREE

Execution Day

I

Το device that had been built in the village square for the execution was known as a guillotine. At the top of a fifteen-foot frame a heavy steel blade was set, and when the executioner released the attached rope, the blade dropped onto the neck of the condemned bent over beneath it. It was believed to be named after its inventor, and while it was said that he himself fell victim to his creation, the veracity of that claim was unknown.

"I've seen them a number of times, but when it comes to be your turn, it's really pretty creepy," Juke said from over by the window.

"It sure as hell is," Sergei agreed, sitting on the edge of the lowest mattress of the triple-decker bunk bed. Gordo was sleeping there. Being a woman, Rosaria was in the cell across from them. They were all in the village jail.

"If I'd known this was gonna happen, I'd have sold a little more of our stock on the side and used the money to really live it up."

"You seem to know all kinds of weird things. Isn't there anything you can do?" Juke said to Sergei, giving the bars across the window a good smack.

"Not a blessed thing. The clowns from the village really went through my stuff good and cleaned me out," Sergei said, showing Juke the palms of both hands. By that, he meant he didn't have anything.

"What'll happen to the goods in our wagon?" he asked.

"If these guys don't pilfer everything, they'll either deliver it somewhere or have someone come get it. Or they'll just say we were hit by bandits and make the whole thing disappear."

"Damn, this is a hell of a mess we've gotten into."

Sergei got up, walked over to the iron bars facing the corridor, and leaned against them.

"Is Rosaria gonna get the ol' *whooosh, ka-chuuung,* too?" he said, striking the back of his neck with the side of his hand.

Juke nodded. "On account of they think she's one of us. If they suspect anyone's ever had anything to do with the Nobility, then they get no mercy; it don't matter if they're injured, a woman, a kid, or what have you."

"Forget about the Nobility. In a case like this, humans are a lot more savage. At least all *they* do is drink your blood. I asked a guy who'd been bitten about it, and he said that partway through it, it felt pretty good. Man, I envy that Gordo. If they chop his head off the way he is now, he'll get an easy death without ever knowing a thing," Sergei muttered, and he actually did sound envious right to the core of his being.

Just then, there was the sound of a door unlocking and the creak of hinges. A number of footsteps could be heard crossing the stone floor and coming their way.

Preceding a couple of sturdy-looking villagers who were apparently the jailers was Mayor Camus. Her pale, aged countenance was in stark contrast to the black satin dress she wore. Needless to say, no one there knew that inside she was actually Dr. Gretchen, poison fiend extraordinaire.

"What a sty!" she said, waving one hand before her nose as she gave Juke and Sergei an icy stare. "Your execution will be conducted precisely at high noon. Just remember: at that exact moment, the guillotine will fall on the neck of one of you."

Though Juke asked her to spare Rosaria, he was met with a laugh.

Glancing out of the corner of her eye at the young lady who slumbered behind the opposite set of bars, she said, "She's one of you—and that's all there is to it."

"You cruel old bitch!" Sergei shouted. His anger was so great that he rattled the bars violently. "Who gains anything by that girl being beheaded? Let her live. If you don't, I'll come back as a ghost and wring the fuck out of that baggy old neck of yours!"

"Such language," Mayor Camus said, grimacing. She looked at him like he was a lowly savage. "We can arrange to have you alone executed earlier. Wouldn't you like to live even a little bit longer?"

"Shut your hole, you lousy murderer," he said, trying to reach through the bars and strangle her.

"Knock it off," Juke said, pulling Sergei back by the shoulders to stop him.

"What kinda scheme are you cooking?" he then asked the mayor.

"Dear me, what a thing to say! I wonder if you're suffering some sort of psychosis before your death."

"You know me, right?" Juke asked the mayor as he stared into her eyes.

"Of course I do."

"I know you, too. You're just like I remember. On the outside, at least."

"Oh, really?"

"You were a hard nut, but you weren't the kind of monster who'd put an innocent girl in the guillotine without doing any checking at all. Are you the real thing?"

"What utter nonsense!" the mayor spat.

Juke didn't catch the turbulence that flashed through her eyes.

Turning to the guards behind her, the mayor told them, "I wish to speak to these men alone. Remain outside until I call for you."

Not surprisingly, the pair of jailers was somewhat bewildered.

"Go!" she asserted coldly, and with that they left.

The door closed. Quickly going over to it, the mayor ran her right hand around its edges, and then touched it to the keyhole. Her hand then went into her gown and pulled out a small earthenware vessel of a muddy brown hue.

"You mean to tell me—" Juke groaned, guessing from that action alone that something wasn't right.

"Be silent," the old woman said as fingers like dead twigs took the lid off the vessel.

A pungent aroma filled the jail, and a scent so dense it seemed to pollute each and every particle of air choked Juke and Sergei.

"G . . . g . . . guards!" they shouted, but their cries gave way to pained wheezing.

"My name is Mayor Camus. But my given name is Dr. Gretchen," the old woman informed them in the alluring voice of a young lady. "I wonder if you might've heard of the woman who poisoned fifty thousand Nobles? At present, all my energies are devoted to ridding the world of the Hunter who calls himself D."

Clinging to the bars, Juke and Sergei had already begun to slide down toward the floor.

Poison it wasn't, but the aroma was that powerful—the scent alone effortlessly pushed their consciousness down into the darkness.

"No matter what you do . . . to us . . . D . . . won't come," Juke said, his voice nearly a death rattle.

"Is that what you believe? I'm of a different opinion," the old woman jeered. The lid was back on the vessel. "I've recently become intimately familiar with his actions on the Frontier for the past few years. The details make my hair stand on end. He's possessed of a cruel and callous mind, the like of which isn't to be found even among the Nobility. He's even mercilessly stabbed into the chest of a young Noble as the child wept and pleaded to be spared. Ordinarily, he would never come to rescue you."

Her wrinkled mouth twisted into a grin. Her lips were as glistening red as rubies.

"However, he is no Noble. His blood is filthy yet hot, like a human's. And so long as that drives his flesh, he won't be able to leave you to your fate. He's certain to come to your rescue. And this village will be his grave."

"Like hell . . . he . . . will," Sergei said, and then he lost consciousness.

"Stay away . . . D," Juke added. His hands came free of the bars, and he toppled in front of a broken chair.

"I took precautions to keep the smell from spilling outside," the mayor remarked. "You've only begun to serve my purposes."

The old woman's unsightly hand reached for the lock; it came free with surprising ease. Catching it so it wouldn't make a sound, she set it down on the floor and entered the trio's cell.

Looking down at the slumped forms of Juke and Sergei, she said, "What a vulgar pose!"

They were bent over not unlike men offering up prayers.

In her hand the old woman held three vessels.

"Each has a different effect. If by some chance you should be rescued, D shall find himself forced to fight me on four fronts. And if you aren't rescued—well, I also have a plan for that contingency."

And then she took the vessels and poured their contents into the mouths of the three men. Three different aromas mixed in the air, creating a mysterious scent.

After she finished with the sleeping Gordo, the old woman put the lock back where it'd been and went to the opposite side of the corridor—where she entered Rosaria's cell.

As she took the lid off a fourth vessel, she felt something on the nape of her neck.

"Huh?"

She turned to look, but there was no one there. Although she'd gotten the feeling she was being watched, apparently she'd been mistaken.

"How unfortunate," said the mayor. "I can't even spare you, Sleeping Beauty."

A golden liquid was poured between the young woman's bloodless lips.

Presently, Mayor Camus grinned like a little girl and called for the guards, but after she'd left, a certain figure appeared without warning in the narrow passageway. It looked for all the world like Rosaria. But wasn't that Rosaria lying there in one of the prison beds?

Though the figure in the corridor gazed quietly but forlornly at her own sleeping self, her eyes suddenly became clear with intent and she started forward without a sound. Ahead of her lay a stone wall. Moving without hesitation, she was just about to hit the wall when the door in it opened and a guard entered. It was time for his appointed rounds. For an instant the two figures overlapped, then parted again. Rosaria had passed right through the man.

"Huh?" the jailer exclaimed, turning around, but by then Rosaria had already disappeared through the stone barrier. Trembling, he slapped himself with both hands. He then went over to Rosaria's cell with long strides, peered in, and got a relieved look on his face.

"Must've drunk too much of those Tudor spirits," the jailer said, speaking aloud the most common explanation when a brush with the unbelievable threatened to fracture the mind. He then slumped back against the bars and let out a deep breath.

The smell that had hung in the air had vanished without a trace.

"I don't know what it is, but I get the feeling this isn't gonna go off well," the man said. Like his life up until now, his tone was small and timid, but somehow he had absolute faith in these words.

II

The leaden clouds that covered the sky at dawn still lazed about as noon approached, showing no intention at all of moving on. Thinking of the ceremony to come and the odious tasks in its wake, some of the men and women in the village had dour expressions, and they were busily scolding the children who ran around like mad. The guillotine that they'd worked through the night to erect towered proudly in the square, with a thick, sharp blade sitting at the top of two wooden uprights. In the simple hut beside it, the executioners sat sipping coffee and looking disdainful.

Ten minutes before the execution, Juke and Sergei were led out of the jail. Rosaria and Gordo had jailers on either side of them to hold them up. The road to the square had been packed on both sides with villagers. Their eyes gleamed with excitement—out on the amusement-starved Frontier, even a grisly death was a wonderful show. As the four condemned and their jailers moved, the people moved with them. Some acted up a bit, swinging axes and knives, but the guards carrying firearms soon put an end to that.

Mayor Camus stood before the guillotine. In her heart of hearts, she didn't really know if D would show up. There'd been no way to let him know for certain the day and time of the execution, and despite what she'd told Juke and Sergei the previous night, she wasn't entirely convinced he would come to their rescue. She'd intentionally postponed the execution one day so that D might learn about it. She couldn't say for sure that this would work . . . which meant that these four would be decapitated for no reason at all. But the terrifying woman wasn't concerned by this. If it came to pass, slaying D by her own hand would become problematic, but she possessed overwhelming self-confidence.

The Duke of Xenon and Grand Duke Mehmet were, of course, thickheaded men who'd attained their positions through brute strength alone. They lacked intellect; this was no longer an era when muscle was pitted against muscle. And the way Dr. Gretchen saw it, D was the same as those two, in which case her own wisdom would more than suffice for slaying him. All that remained was to cross paths with him. She'd think of another way to take care of him when she did.

The four prisoners reached the bottom of the scaffold. The hue of the clouds seemed to grow a good deal duller and heavier.

"There's no point in a whole lot of useless chatter. Let's get right to it," declared Mayor Camus. "First will be—"

"Me," Juke said, puffing his chest.

"We'll start with the girl."

"You bitch—what are you, a Noble?" Juke shouted as he tried to grab hold of the old woman, but the jailers promptly wrestled him down. "Kill me first! Do the woman later."

"This is hardly the place for a display of manly compassion," Mayor Camus said frostily, taking the chin of the limp Rosaria in hand and raising her face. "Fast asleep. It would be best for her if we got this over quickly, while she remains so. Set her up."

"Stop!"

Juke and Sergei continued to protest, but they were held hand and foot, and there was nothing they could do as Rosaria went up the wooden stairs, supported by a man on either side. There were thirteen stairs.

On reaching the top, one of the jailers lifted the upper lunette, a wooden bar that had an opening in the center of its lower side. An eight-inch-thick log that had been brought out expressly for this purpose was set in the hollow in the lower beam, and then the upper one was lowered again. After locking both halves in place, the jailer quickly made his way over to a wooden lever.

A stir went through the crowd like a wave, and it brought a silence that spread across the square.

Well aware of the spectators' gaze, the jailer waited a moment before pulling the lever. The sound of the falling blade mixed with that of friction from the rope. When the protruding section of the log was cleanly bisected and fell into the basket below, a cry of excitement went up from the crowd, which was clearly impressed.

Raising one hand to acknowledge the throng, the jailer went over to his partner—who'd been drilling him with an envious stare—and with his help bent Rosaria over before the lunettes. The entire process of setting her in place in the same manner as the log was carried out in an extremely professional manner.

Once more, silence returned to the square. Nothing had disrupted the event yet, and everyone hoped the same could be said for the rest of it.

Needless to say, lookouts had been posted around the village, their eyes agleam to keep from missing even the smallest thing. Not so much as an insect was to get through.

The jailer's hand grabbed hold of the lever. He gave it a rough pull. An atrocious whine dropped from heaven toward the earth.

This was the moment.

The guillotine floated up into the air, scaffold and all. Even the supports that were sunk in the ground pulled free with ease, and the soil they sent flying followed right along after them. A black hole had suddenly appeared in the sky fifteen feet above the guillotine. Before the villagers had even noticed it, the hole began sucking up everything in the area: the guillotine, its blade, Rosaria, and even the jailers on the platform. Still not knowing what was happening, Juke and Sergei also floated up into the air. Unwilling to relent, their jailers started after the men.

Mayor Camus alone saw what was really happening.

"A space eater?" she muttered.

Grand Duke Mehmet alone could control them. Was he interfering with the execution?

"Don't let them—" the mayor began to shout, but she gave up before she got to the word *escape*.

Not even the space eater in question knew where its hole would lead. The end of time or the bowels of the earth—wherever it went, anything sucked into it now would be lost forever.

When her thoughts had progressed to this point, she finally began to act like a leader, shouting, "Everybody, run away! You'll be sucked into the hole!"

Before her words could serve as a guide for those dashing around aimlessly, they were instead drawn up along with the villagers being sucked toward the void.

In the woods, about five hundred yards from the outer wall of the village, a figure in black sailed down from a particularly tall tree like a mystic bird. More than the way he landed without a sound, it was the way the hem of his coat spread like an ebony blossom just before he did so that made his identity clear at a glance. It was D. In the kingdom of intertwined shadow and light that was the woods, he was a dazzling figure in black—and the figure beside him in equally gorgeous hues watched him with a suspicious yet enraptured gaze. Her expression seemed to inquire, *What do you intend to do?*

Asking nothing and being told nothing, Lady Ann had merely followed along diligently after D. Though D had said it would be better to have the girl around, he made no attempt to make use of her. And that actually hurt the darling little girl.

"Five seconds to go," a hoarse voice from the vicinity of his left hand told him. D's left hand was held up against his chest with the palm facing out. "Three . . . Two . . . One . . . Now!"

A small lump shot from the palm of his hand. A little bug. Flying a good fifteen feet through the air, it landed on a bush and devoured itself.

It was at that moment that a hole opened like a lazy black swirl. The tiny gap grew larger, and a second later the most incredible thing flew out of it. What should make the earth shudder and smash the grass flat but a brand-new guillotine that stuck into the dirt at an angle! Following that, people quickly piled on the ground one on top of another, forming a small mound.

"Exactly forty people," the left hand reported, sounding quite pleased. "Oh, there they are. Rosaria, Juke, and Sergei. Why, even Gordo's safe and sound. That was flawless timing. I hope you appreciate it."

D ignored the hand. He squatted down beside Rosaria to take her pulse and check her pupils, and then he moved on to Juke.

After seeing to all four, D put the lot of them over his shoulders— they had to be between six and seven hundred pounds. Of course, this sort of thing must've been natural for a Noble, because Lady Ann didn't look at all surprised.

Not even glancing at the remaining villagers, D put the village behind them. After all, these were people who'd been on the edge of their seats waiting to watch a girl get decapitated.

Outside the village a cargo wagon and horses were waiting— they'd been purchased early that morning at a neighboring village. Putting the four people in the vehicle, D got into the driver's seat and took the reins. The team of four cyborg horses ran as if entranced by the bewitching beauty of their master.

"How did you manage to do that?" Lady Ann asked from between the driver's seat and where the other four lay, her head cocked to one side. She was referring to how he'd gotten the four of them to appear from the hole the space eater had chewed through space.

Strangely enough, she got an answer quite quickly. From D's left hand.

"Everything sucked into a hole created by a space eater ends up flying off into the depths of time and space. It takes precisely ten seconds for that to happen. It's exactly the same as the way a person or animal needs time to chew before they swallow their food. And if another space eater opens a hole in a different spot at the instant the first reaches the time limit, everything that was sucked up automatically gets blown out through the new one. However, it takes superhuman skill to do that. I take it you saw the last three or four villagers who came out. They were pretty much reduced to protoplasm. Well, the good news is he was only interested in these four anyway."

As soon as the left hand's lengthy discourse ended, Lady Ann muttered pensively, "Controlling space eaters, of all things . . ."

The two bugs in question were ones Grand Duke Mehmet had launched at the newly risen D back in the ruins. D had bisected them instead of dodging them, and by funneling the power of his left hand into the bugs, he'd managed to bring them back to life. This was possible in part because the bugs had an inherently tenacious life force. Nothing up to this point was particularly strange, but space eaters were not easily trained—it was impossible to predict when one would begin to devour itself. On account of this, the number of incidents where people trying to catch the bugs had been sucked instead into their holes was innumerable. In addition, no one but the most accomplished insect wranglers would ever attempt to keep and breed them. The techniques of working with space eaters were a closely guarded secret that was spoken of only in the world of darkness. Yet D had done it easily enough.

"How could you . . ." Lady Ann began, her eyes and cheeks colored with admiration.

"His old man's special, you see. There's pretty much nothing any Noble can do that he can't. Gaaaah!"

The voice died out there, sounding like it'd been strangled, and after a short time had passed, D unballed his fist.

In the meantime, and even after that, Lady Ann's doll-like eyes swam with curiosity and anxiety as she pondered something. With a sort of sudden awakening, she then said, "You can do anything the Nobility can, and your father is special . . . Could it be you . . . Your highness is . . ."

As she murmured this, the wagon swerved off the road and started down into the valley on the right-hand side, its tires leaving ruts behind them. Keeping an eye on the steadiness of the cyborg horses that galloped down a steep and narrow path without any sign of danger, Lady Ann soon realized that it was the influence of D at the reins that allowed them to do so, and the girl's eyes flickered with a deeper gleam of admiration.

Between trees that arched their branches like the legs of gigantic insects, the toppled ruins of a stone fortress seemed to lie humbly under the protection of the boughs. With this as their backdrop, they came before long to a place where there was the roar of a torrent and the dance of white spray. It was a waterfall.

The cyborg horses crashed right into the curtain of water, which was easily three hundred feet high and thirty feet wide, sending water splashing wildly before they reached the massive cavern that lay behind the falls.

III

With an area of at least ten thousand square feet and a ceiling some sixty feet high, the immense cavern was something Sergei had heard about before. He said it was the remains of an extremely ancient civilization he'd read about in old documents—a civilization that antedated the Nobility. It was said to be hidden behind a large waterfall and that from long ago those living nearby had been afraid to approach it, so he maintained that it should remain exactly as it'd been for the last ten thousand years. Of course, D had discovered this place because of his ultrakeen senses, but the presence of the cavern was extremely difficult to detect from outside—even at close range. While General Gaskell's assassins might be a different story, this would most definitely keep them safe from any pursuers from the village.

The interior was just a vast space without a hint of any ancient civilization.

On seeing the strangely smooth surface of the ground and walls, the left hand remarked, "This was melted. Must've been blasted with an ultraheat ray of more than a hundred thousand degrees for over a minute. That'd be the Nobility's doing. They tried to completely wipe out every trace of any civilization older than their own."

For a while D rode around inspecting the cave on a cyborg horse he'd unhitched from the wagon, and then he returned to the vehicle and laid the four humans out on level ground. When he put his left hand against their foreheads, Juke and Sergei woke up immediately.

D turned his gaze to Lady Ann.

"Yes?" she said eagerly. "Can I do anything for you?"

Though the look he gave her was cold as ice, to the girl it seemed for all the world like a loving glance from the man of her dreams.

"Get him up," D said, tossing his chin in Gordo's direction.

"Of course, I'll be happy to," she replied.

"She can set him right?" Sergei asked with a dull expression of astonishment.

"Why'd you let it go until now?" Juke asked, blinking.

"If I'd told her to fix him before, do you think she'd have done it?" D said to them. "If I'd tried to force her, she may have taken her own life."

"Precisely!" Lady Ann cried out. Her voice quivered with excitement. "A Noble would rather plunge into the fires of hell than live with the disgrace of having benefited their foe. Had I been forced to save the very opponent I'd defeated, I would've chosen destruction right then and there. Ah, D, you understand me all too well!"

As the girl folded her pale and dainty hands in front of her chest with satisfaction, Juke and Sergei stared at her, dumbfounded, and then shifted their gaze to D.

"Be quick about it," D told her with his usual gruffness, and then he put his left hand to Rosaria's brow.

"It's bad, as I suspected. This is a curse," the hoarse voice said. "The only thing you can do is finish off the one who did this to her. In other words—Gaskell."

Although Ann had listened to the left hand in silence, she inquired somewhat angrily, "Just who is this woman, anyway?"

"There's no way you would know her," D replied.

Ann shook her head from side to side, saying, "No, this woman came while you were asleep back in the ruins. She told you about today's execution."

"A doppelgänger?" his left hand muttered.

Such creatures weren't particularly rare on the Frontier. However, most of them were projections that committed malicious acts against the wishes of the person they mimicked—in many cases they were that person's negative side. If this applied to Rosaria, then would bringing her along on this trip be tantamount to setting out with a belly full of poison?

Perhaps Lady Ann had reached the same conclusion, because for the first time in an age, a hint of cruelty well suited to the girl flitted across her lips.

"This is a dangerous woman. I shall dispose of her," the girl said.

Her right hand had already been raised to strike, and scythelike nails stretched from her fingertips. They whistled through the air toward the windpipe of the sleeping woman, only to halt in midair with a sound like a hard slap. The black-gloved hand that held her wrist belonged to D.

"Kindly unhand me," the girl said, gnashing her teeth and writhing with frustration, an intense look on her face. It was the face of a woman out of her mind with love. It was nauseatingly ugly and beautiful beyond measure at the same time.

"How ridiculous!" she fumed.

As soon as the Hunter's left hand touched the scruff of her neck, Lady Ann collapsed on the spot.

"I won't allow this . . ." the fearsome little darling muttered as if goading herself on, her shoulders heaving with each breath. "Any woman who tries to come near you . . . I can't allow to live . . ."

How did the beautiful Hunter feel listening to the girl's groans of brutal honesty? Not even glancing at her, he said, "Wake up Gordo."

He then turned to Juke and Sergei and said, "What do you want to do?"

"What do you mean?"

The two looked at each other.

"You don't have any cargo to deliver to the other villages now. And if we part company, Gaskell won't be after you any longer."

"Good plan. Let's do that," Juke said with a grin, but then he got serious again. "Are you still under contract with us?"

"Of course."

"Then help us out here. We're gonna go get our wagon and merchandise back."

"Hey, hold on a minute!" Sergei cried out in a tone that could only be described as tragic. "We're going back to that village? That's the craziest thing I've ever heard!"

"We're transporters. We get looted and nearly killed, and you think we can call it a day? Those other villages are waiting on pins and needles for that cargo to arrive."

"Yeah, but—"

"Say your daughter is dying. Medical supplies from the Capital could save her. But a bunch of useless transporters come along, heads hung low, crying about how all their goods got stolen and begging forgiveness. You think you're just gonna clap 'em on the back and tell 'em, 'Oh, that's okay'?"

The man had a piercing gaze trained on Sergei, who scratched his head uncomfortably.

"I get you. You're perfectly right."

"Damn straight he is!"

Turning full speed in the direction of this heavy voice, Sergei let out a joyous cry of, "Gordo!"

"Hey, you came to?" Juke said, following Sergei's lead and running over to his compatriot.

"Yeah. As you can see, I'm right as rain!"

Now sitting up, the bearded man smiled grandly as he flexed his muscles.

"Hey, Sergei!" he called out to his colleague.

"What is it?" Sergei replied, but no sooner had he brought his face closer than a sudden punch landed noisily against his jaw.

Though he dropped to his knees, he somehow managed to keep his torso upright, nursing his chin as he shouted, "What the hell was that for?"

"Regret what you said now, you big idiot? Any courier who's more worried about his own safety than the goods he's carrying is a waste of skin. And that's the kind of talk you were spilling a second ago. You ever try to turn tail again, and you'd better be ready for the consequences!"

"Okay! I get it! I get it already!" Sergei shouted with a pained smile. "Well, if the two of you aren't just brimming with a sense of duty! You'll never live to a ripe old age."

"Neither will you, dummy," the other two sneered back.

"How about giving some thought to how to retrieve it?" D said, his words bringing them all back to their senses.

And then, behind the roaring falls, a visage so handsome it seemed to be from another world and three relatively average faces alternately spoke in hushed seriousness or collided in heated debate, finally coming to a consensus when the light outside was fading in hue.

"I wonder if he's coming?"

"No, he won't come."

"Oh, yes, he will."

These three opinions mixed in the air, melting together as two travelers and an old woman stared intently at each other's faces.

Although they were disguised as middle-aged travelers, there could be no containing the intensity of their eyes or the inhuman stateliness that spilled from every inch of them. It was Grand Duke Mehmet and Roland, the Duke of Xenon. An hour earlier they'd left the village, which was in chaos following the incident with the space eater, and climbed to the top of a hill to the north. The silhouettes of birds skimmed across a sky deep blue with the approaching dusk. Their conversation focused on the fate of D and the transporters, and now the trio was of differing opinions.

"Why would they come back to the village where they nearly lost their lives just for their wagon and its cargo?" Grand Duke Mehmet said. Not only his lips but his whole face as well twisted from time to time due to the pain that shot through his arms and back—apparently the pain of the gigantic marionette losing its limbs had been transmitted to his own body.

"He'll come," the Duke of Xenon asserted. "I hear that for those who live on the Frontier, death is preferable to the shame of not fulfilling your professional obligations. The way I see it, they'll definitely return to get their wagon and their goods."

"You seem well informed as to the human way of life," said the old woman—Mayor Camus, who was in fact Dr. Gretchen—as she glanced briefly at the Duke of Xenon's face. It was a sarcastic look, and an equally sarcastic tone. "But this time it serves you well. I also believe the humans will come back. I have no idea why D is traveling with them, and he may be another matter entirely, but the three men will return."

"If they do, then good," Grand Duke Mehmet said, looking up. "The Duke of Xenon and I waited outside the village since early this morning. And we swore to ourselves that if D or anyone working on his behalf were to come, *this* time we would deliver him unto death. But who would've thought—I mean, who could've imagined he'd do it in such a manner?"

The grand duke removed the patch from his right eye.

In the direction of his gaze a number of birds circled and soared. Suddenly, one of them stopped beating its wings and went into a steep dive, as if enamored of the ground. Less than a second later it was joined by a second—and a third. Once the poor birds had disappeared somewhere in the distant woods, Grand Duke Mehmet finally let out a breath and put the eye patch back on.

The power of a look alone—the murderous intent that radiated from his eyes—knocked birds in flight from the sky. This was a perfectly natural occurrence for a member of the Nobility, as was evinced by the fact that the expressions of his two fellow Nobles didn't change in the slightest.

But the ferocity of the grand duke's rage and the reason for his mood were painfully clear. They'd been bested using space eaters only the grand duke could control. Moreover, he could only imagine that the bugs in question were the same ones D had cut in two. If so, the responsibility for this tremendous setback all lay with him—Grand Duke Mehmet. That was the source of the rage that caused him to knock birds dead from the sky.

"Though I understand your anger, there is no need for the two of you to engage him once again," Mayor Camus/Dr. Gretchen said, gazing at the two men.

The indignant looks she drew from them were a response to the undercurrent of derision in her words.

"What do you mean by that?" Roland, the Duke of Xenon, inquired softly.

"What I mean is that I've already taken measures. Measures only I might take."

The men exchanged glances. Though each was an incomparable warrior, they needed no demonstration of this murderess's skill with poisons. The clouds of discomfort that welled up in their hearts began to take shape, telling them that this woman, of all people, might be able to do it alone.

"What kind of measures?" the duke was prompted to ask, which in itself revealed his state of mind.

"It's a secret," Dr. Gretchen replied, true to form, and then she looked up at the rolling blue sky and stretched. "If D should fail to return, then there is someone already under my spell—and that spell is eating its way into them. Ah, the sunlight we cursed for so long feels so good today! There's something to be said for the daytime, isn't there?"

One might even say there was an innocent joy in her eyes, but then those same eyes abruptly narrowed as she said, "Oh, there goes a flock of birds. Winged psychopomps, I believe. They're flying twice as high as the ones the grand duke struck down with his glance just now. Can you do the same to *them*, Grand Duke Mehmet?"

The man with the look that killed turned away in a snit. Not surprisingly, it was beyond his ability.

"And you, Duke of Xenon?"

As she asked him this, the traveler in red hauled back with his right arm as if to hurl a javelin. At some point, grotesque armor had come to sheathe him from the elbow down to the tips of his fingers. He swung his empty right hand. But the sound that ripped through the air wasn't that of a hand.

It rose higher. And higher. And higher still.

"You scored a hit," Dr. Gretchen said with squinted eyes.

About twenty seconds later, it became abundantly clear that a number of the avian shapes were falling. They dropped. Ignoring the rotation of the earth, they landed right in the center of a circle formed by the trio. Roughly a dozen winged psychopomps had been pierced through the breast and out the back by an unseen spear high above the earth.

"Remarkable," Dr. Gretchen said with a smile. And remaining in Mayor Camus's form, she said, "But that was only fifteen of them. From six miles away, the Duke of Xenon's spear could do no better than fifteen birds out of a hundred."

She punctuated this with a haughty laugh.

"You seriously intend to say you could do better, Dr. Gretchen?" the Duke of Xenon asked, flames of outrage covering him from head to foot like a suit.

"But of course, my good duke—allow me to demonstrate."

The old woman raised her left hand. A golden ring set with a purple stone glittered on her ring finger. When she flicked the stone up, a mistlike strand rose from the setting and climbed into the air.

Ten seconds passed. Twenty.

Grand Duke Mehmet and Roland, the Duke of Xenon, exchanged despicable grins that hardly suited the vaunted Nobility. They knew what Dr. Gretchen was trying to do. However, there was no way any poison on earth could reach thirty thousand feet into the atmosphere without dispersing. Especially not when what had risen from her ring had been a gas.

The smiles of the pair vanished. For Dr. Gretchen had looked up at the heavens. And laughed.

As she laughed, she made an easy leap, and then a second—and had bounded thirty feet away.

"Stand back!" she told them.

Grand Duke Mehmet made a leap that carried him thirty feet as well.

And a second later, all over and around the Duke of Xenon—who'd been left behind—there was the successive thudding of impacts like the crashing of angry waves, and the Nobleman was shrouded in a crimson fog. The Duke of Xenon had been enveloped by his exoskeleton, but suddenly his shoulders and head were struck and countless chunks went flying everywhere. Beaks. Heads. Eyes. Talons. Wings. Feathers. They were birds. Having plummeted thirty thousand feet, the birds noisily thudded against the duke and the ground. The fog was blood.

"That's all of them aside from your fifteen," Dr. Gretchen said off in the distance. "I've also arranged to use this virulent poison against D—it'd been dispersed by the wind, dissolved into the air, and diluted to but a millionth of its normal strength when it reached those unfortunate birds."

The doctor spun around.

"Run if you like. Hide under a rock somewhere. First I shall cover the ground for three miles with the corpses of anything that flies."

And just as the old woman had said, for the next few seconds birds, insects, and reptiles—anything that flew—dropped by the tens of thousands to blanket the ground around them with their corpses.

Mistress of Toxins

CHAPTER 2

I

Midnight. Shadowy figures approached the fence around the village—one at the main gate and two on the west side. The footsteps of the one at the gate rang out, while those of the pair to the west made not a sound.

On noticing those footfalls, the villager in the watchtower at the gate turned his searchlight in their direction. A special lens magnified the modest light of a candle a million times, throwing a beam that picked out the form of this nocturnal intruder starkly.

"D!" was all the villager said before he froze.

Painted with that white light, the young man in black swayed like a mirage, glowing, his gorgeous features like something that couldn't possibly be of this world. Seeing how D advanced without saying a word, the villager in the watchtower finally threw the switch on the siren.

The wail that split the stillness of the night reached the ears of the mayor and the two travelers at her house.

"He's here!"

"I knew he'd come."

After three short blasts, the sound died out.

"It's D. Apparently he's come alone," Mayor Camus said, rising from her chair with a grace hardly expected from someone of her age.

Tobacco smoke swayed in the air. It came from Grand Duke Mehmet's cigar.

"Well—shall we go, then?" the Duke of Xenon said, rising as well. "As per our draw, I'll face him first. Which is fortunate, since it'll give me a chance to make him tell me where my daughter is before I finish him off."

"I'm next, then?" Grand Duke Mehmet said, using a china ashtray to crush out the cigar he held. "Then I shall go conceal myself where no one will find me. If you'll excuse me."

He relied on an enormous, immortal puppet to do battle. His body was hidden while he controlled it. Because an attack against his true self would be a serious matter, it was quite natural that he kept his location a secret even from his own colleagues—particularly from colleagues he couldn't trust.

As the two Noblemen headed for the door, white smoke crept around their feet and enveloped them.

"Too bad, Dr. Gretchen," Grand Duke Mehmet said with a despicable laugh. "We realized that you would never wait to go third, and that you would try to make us inhale poison to stop us. So before coming here, we had General Gaskell's physician put something in our blood to counteract poisons. There's nothing you can do to us any longer."

The grand duke's body staggered forward, as if pulled on a line.

"This . . . this can't be . . ."

First Grand Duke Mehmet fell, and then the Duke of Xenon dropped right on top of him.

Looking down at the pair with her old woman's mask, the mistress of toxins laughed like a bell.

"The general's physician, you say? You think someone who isn't even a specialist could know everything about my beloved poisons? What you just inhaled is newly concocted. No antidote will work on it." Baring her pale throat with a laugh, she continued, "Now, then—I, the poisoning fiend Dr. Gretchen, am going off to dispose of D, the Hunter of Nobility, in accordance with the wishes of our Sacred Ancestor."

And then the infamous poisoner who wore the guise of an old woman stepped lightly through the door and out into the world of night. Into the kingdom of the Nobility, where battle and life and death all waited.

Juke and Sergei were the pair of figures who were climbing over the west side of the fence while the siren was going off.

"I wonder if D will be okay."

"Get your own job done before you start worrying about anyone else. Where are the wagon and our cargo?"

Pondering Juke's question for a second, Sergei said, "Where they store all their goods."

In unison they said, "The western warehouse!" These men had visited this village several times before.

While they ran from shadow to shadow, as if stitching the darkness together, Sergei said, "That little princess—we left her behind, but she's got me worried."

"Hey, Gordo's keeping an eye on her."

"That's what worries me—what Gordo might do."

Gordo didn't know how many times he'd already pressed the muzzle of his gun to Lady Ann's brow or the back of her head. It wasn't just because this fearsome little girl had left him completely incapacitated until a short time earlier; it was also because she was obviously a member of the Nobility.

Why am I letting her live? This question, too, had risen in his mind more times than he could count. *Because D said it would keep the Nobles from attacking us.* That was certainly true, and he agreed. However, while reason was satisfied, emotion wasn't. The fear of the Nobility that was branded into human DNA commanded him to blow the angelic face off the innocent little girl who lay at his feet.

You know, reason told him coldly, *a Noble won't die from a gunpowder weapon. You could blow her head off or shoot her heart out a hundred times, but they'd be back again as long as the dark of night persisted.*

He'd have to do something else to take the life out of her once and for all. Drive a wooden stake or steel blade into her heart, or cut her head off. And Gordo had tried that countless times, too. Pulling the machete from his belt, he'd tried to sever the girl's head. He'd tried to stab her through the heart. As he drew his machete, he'd felt the weapon's formidable weight as he raised it over his head. He raised it high. And every time he did, he got the same feeling in his hands. The feeling he'd gotten jabbing a stake into that woman's chest years ago.

Die! Die! he must've muttered or shouted countless times. He ordered his nerves and muscles to obey as he grew slick with sweat. Perhaps less than twelve inches lay between life and death.

From beneath the overwhelming voice that pressured him to take the girl's life, the tone of reason snaked out, thin but strong as steel. *You stabbed the woman who killed your mother and your brothers and sisters,* it said. *Just ask the palm of your hand. Ask it how it felt the moment you drove a stake into that soft flesh.*

"I can't!"

Gordo had no choice but to lower the machete he'd raised again.

As D and two of the transporter's compatriots were leaving, Lady Ann had asked to accompany them, but D had driven his fist into her solar plexus and knocked her out. She'd since been bound hand and foot with wire, and a blindfold covered her eyes. Her limbs were tied to guard against her monstrous strength. The blindfold was intended to negate the powers of mesmerism the Nobility possessed.

"I just can't do it. Guess I've got no choice but to wait," Gordo murmured, wiping his sweat off, but due to the roar of the falls, he couldn't even hear himself very well.

Out of the corner of his eye, he saw something move. Lady Ann. Before Gordo's wide and horrified eyes, the little vampire lady whom D's blow had rendered unconscious was slowly but smoothly righting herself.

In a lethargic voice she said, "I can't see."

Her whole body tensed. Power coursed into her arms, still secured behind her back. However, the steely line didn't break.

"I can't move," she said in a voice that was terribly sweet and unsettling at the same time.

In one corner of his mind, Gordo thought, *Is that how Nobles are?* Even the roar of the falls disappeared when the girl's voice rang out.

"Who's done this to me? Are you there?"

For some reason, he responded. "Yeah."

"I knew someone was there."

The girl's words turned Gordo's heart to ice.

"Please, take this blindfold off of me," the girl entreated him sadly. "I beg of you. I can't see anything."

"I can't. And don't move."

"Why won't you heed me? If you toy with me, you should fear the consequences."

"Shut up."

"I beg of you," Lady Ann repeated. A little nasal, her voice was that of a cute little ten-year-old girl. Even without having seen her face, he could've envisioned the watery blue depths of her eyes, the gold of her hair, and her full cheeks and lips, all from that voice. "Please! I beg of you!"

Gordo was completely aware of what he was doing. Wiping his sweat away before rubbing his hands against his pants, he could hear every creak of his joints as he walked toward Lady Ann. Oh, why hadn't D gagged her, too? His hands went into action. He was moving toward the girl, toward the knot in her blindfold. Why was he untying it?

"Thank you," she said, Gordo's face reflected in the watery blue of her eyes—and rising from their watery depths were malice and a savage hunger.

II

Even beneath the unchanging sea of clouds, D could see as distinctly as if it were midday the old woman who came out through the gates. It was unclear if the Hunter found anything strange about the absence of the two Nobles who should've accompanied her—Grand Duke Mehmet and Roland, the Duke of Xenon. However, his face, in all its unearthly beauty, was trained on his approaching foe, as still as the air on a harsh winter's night.

"I was wondering if you know who I am?" the mayor asked.

"What happened to the other two?" D inquired. To this young man, the names of those he had to slay had no meaning.

"I put them to sleep. It is I that shall slay you—Dr. Gretchen!" she said, her voice no longer that of an old woman, but rather the honey-dripping tone of a temptress.

"When will they get up?"

"That will depend on their constitutions. Perhaps they already have. Perhaps they never will. They inhaled enough poison to kill a human being ten times over. If you want to take care of all of us in one fell swoop, this is your chance."

D went into action—he seemed to share that sentiment. As he dashed forward, he drew his blade. The instant Dr. Gretchen's body entered the deadly arc it described, another death would be decorated with fresh blood.

However, when D was about fifteen feet from the villainess, he pitched forward. Sticking his sword into the ground, he tried to use it as a lever to pull himself up again, but his lower half crumbled feebly. Black beads formed on his face, leaving threadlike trails as they began to stream down it. They were blood—lifeblood that gushed from D's pores.

"Did you get your four friends back safely? How accommodating of you," jeered a figure that his night vision revealed to be a woman of dazzling beauty. "I made them drink my poisons. Without knowing it, all four of them became poison people. It's perfectly natural that not even you knew it. After all, there wasn't anything out of the ordinary about any of them. However, you breathed in what they exhaled, and little by little it collected in your body, causing a delicate chemical reaction. Adding one last poison will cause the same reaction as an immortal Noble exposed to sunlight."

D's forehead split open horizontally, and from it a blinding light shone on the gate. His shoulder split. His upper arm broke open, and then his chest and abdomen ruptured. Light pierced his clothes, shining down at the earth and up into the void, transforming D into an anthropomorphic sun in black raiment.

"When subjected to the Daybreak effect of my poisons, even the greatest of the Greater Nobility screamed in agony and pleaded with me to kill them. How about you?"

Not answering her, D tumbled forward. The hand that still gripped his sword split apart from wrist to elbow, unleashing a new light. The light grew much more intense, swallowing the young man in black. He was literally a sun that had been born to the night.

Perhaps it was unavoidable that the mother of that sun should laugh mockingly, midday in the midst of darkness—but even as this was happening, Dr. Gretchen's laughter ceased. The glow had continued to intensify, cutting through the defensive shield General Gaskell had given her and searing her flesh with the feverish heat of midday.

"How is this possible?" she cried out in amazement, as every place the light touched her grew white hot. She was gripped with the fear of having her immortal flesh charred right down to the marrow of her bones. The light continued to envelop the poisoning murderess.

"Aaaaah! Begone!" she exclaimed, but when she tried to leap away, both her legs shattered at the knee. The joints were shrouded in white flames. Her protective shield had been broken.

"Impossible! This can't be! Help me!"

Dr. Gretchen fought madly to extinguish the flames. However, every time she struck them, white light spread from that spot, and new flames shot from the hand she'd brought down on it.

"How—how can this be? I—I'm burning!" she cried as her whole body was wrapped in light like some sacred sculpture. It was said that, in protest against the actions of their fellow man, human holy men had once set themselves aflame—but rather than a saint, this was a demonic Noble in agony.

Just as the hellish torment was about to drive her out of her mind, a needle of wood whined through the air from the light that had enveloped D and pierced Dr. Gretchen through the heart.

"Gaaaah!"

When she unleashed that death rattle, the skin and flesh had already melted from her body, leaving bare bones. Yet her mouth moved and she formed words, saying, "Why? Why doesn't my Daybreak have any effect? Somebody, please tell me. Ooooh!"

Her last cry was an expression not of surprise but of horror. The source of the light that was incinerating the queen of toxins rapidly lost its color, retreating as if to avoid some counterattack by the darkness, while from it stepped a figure in black. It was a man descended from Nobility who feared nothing save the day, yet who'd been turned into a source of sunlight and had still come back from the dead—D.

"You . . . Are you stronger . . . than even the greatest of the Greater Nobility? You, no more than . . . a dhampir. A filthy half-breed . . ."

The burning murderess raised a right hand reduced to bone. What did she intend to do with the poison in the jar? Turning, she aimed the container at the village fence. The contents of the jar were a virulent toxin that would become an odorless and colorless gas the second it made contact with the air, suffocating every living creature in a six-mile radius.

"Just watch. Here is my final gift to the world!"

The doctor threw it with all her might, but she was now nothing but a skeleton. As the jar limned a gentle arc that would carry it over the fence, a white light followed it. A rough wooden needle deflected the jar without breaking it. As it fell toward the ground, a hand in a black glove caught it. Though his glove and coat were both shredded, D's hand demonstrated untold force and power. When she saw him put the jar away in his coat, Dr. Gretchen's skeleton chattered its largely melted teeth and jaws with regret, and then it lost all cohesion and clattered to the ground. The bones quickly lost their shape, turning to dust. Yet her voice could still be heard.

"How did you . . ."

"Someone told me what you'd done," D replied.

Did he pity the woman in her frustration? Or had her tactics been so utterly inhuman as to garner a certain respect?

"Who . . . was it?" said the one bone that remained on the mound of dust—the skull. Its vocal cords and tongue had long since turned to dust, yet it seemed to produce the voice from sheer tenacity.

"It was Rosaria," D answered.

To be precise, it had been the *other* Rosaria—a spirit or a doppelgänger that had appeared before D as he watched the preparations for the execution before dawn from a tree, and had told the Hunter that Dr. Gretchen had made the four of them drink poison.

"You used the same trick once on a certain Greater Noble. I remembered that."

"Impossible . . . Why, that was . . . ten thousand years ago! Besides . . . how did you make an antidote?"

"I didn't."

The skull's teeth came to a dead stop. "What I did to you . . . would burn a Noble down to the bone. Because it turns you into the sun . . . no one can withstand it. Yet how did you manage this . . . without any antidote? Why . . . the only one who's ever endured that was our Sacred Ancestor . . ."

Her voice petered out there, and then came back again. This time it was so faint, it didn't seem it would even reach human ears.

"Now . . . I finally see . . . D . . . your face . . . I've seen it somewhere. It can't be . . . You can't be . . . Your highness is . . ."

After watching the last remaining bone lose its shape and turn to dust, D headed for the main gate on foot. Two foes he needed to deal with still remained in the village.

When D was about six feet from the gate, a flash of black light angled up out of the ground. Taking D through the solar plexus, it came out again though the back of his neck. Not making a sound, D kept his left hand in his pocket as he grabbed the long spear with his right and tried to pull it out through his back. Just then, a second spear burst from the earth. D grabbed that with his right hand as well, but its steel head slipped through his hand, tying his solar plexus and neck together again.

Laughter rose from the ground. And as it rose, black earth flew away to reveal a gigantic exoskeleton. Roland, the Duke of Xenon.

"I was watching your battle all along from underground. As Dr. Gretchen herself said, that poison wasn't terribly potent. And as I watched, I noticed something. D—you can't see, can you?"

Their wagon was indeed in the warehouse. And its cargo was still loaded. The only reason they thought it wasn't a trap was because this village had had so much trouble lately, and the pair decided the townspeople hadn't had time to break down the load yet. They were half right. Thanks to the accuracy of their deduction, all their hardships had been banished from the brains of the two men, and that was where the danger lay. Yes—it was a trap. The pair did a quick yet thorough investigation, but there didn't seem to be any problem. Nor was there any sign of anyone in hiding.

"All right," Juke said when he was sure they were in the clear. Sergei was overjoyed.

Silence had returned to the darkness outside. What kind of unearthly battle was D locked in with their foes?

With D, their decoy, coming right up to the front door, the pair of transporters planned to make off with their wagon and cargo while the Hunter kept the villagers occupied. The plan was a simple, tried-and-true classic, and it seemed it would come off perfectly. They were concerned about D, but he'd told them to take off as soon as they'd done their part.

Juke climbed up onto the roof, and Sergei got in the driver's seat.

"We're gonna tear straight out of here!"

But as soon as Sergei took up the reins, a fourteen-foot-tall figure came in through the warehouse entrance.

"Holy crap!"

"What the hell is that?"

That was all they could say as the giant's smooth movements placed it in front of the wagon. When its enormous face turned in their direction, Sergei started to draw the rivet gun D had procured at the neighboring village.

"Don't," the face told him, and he froze. After all, the face was more than double the size of any person's.

"Just who are you?" Juke, who was tougher than Sergei, asked. He had his firearm out on the roof.

"My name is Grand Duke Mehmet—I'm one of General Gaskell's guests. Come now—if you fire that, the villagers are sure to come running. What's more, shooting me won't do any good."

"Then what do you want?" Sergei asked from the driver's seat. He was getting used to the large face. No longer afraid, he was puzzled.

"Nothing in particular. I don't care about the two of you. Ordinarily, it wouldn't matter to me whether I simply let you go or if I smashed you flat. Which shall it be?"

"I'd have to go with the one where you say, 'On your way, guys.' "

Juke nodded at Sergei's reply.

"However . . ." Until this point, there'd been something humorous about the grand duke's expression, but suddenly it became that of a merciless Noble. "I can use the two of you—to slay D. Gretchen, that sly minx, tricked me, and by the time I'd woken up, Roland had also, so perhaps it was fortunate that I noticed the two of you out in front of this warehouse."

"I'm not sure exactly what you're talking about, but you'd best hurry up and go. You're just gonna fall further behind at this rate."

"Oh, I don't mind. No matter how impressive Dr. Gretchen or Roland may be, I don't think either of them alone is a match for that Hunter. With his swordsmanship and his bearing—I'm afraid to say I don't believe in the least that I can face him on my own."

The huge face twisted into an evil grin. Eyes as big as fists reflected the faces of the two transporters.

"Yes, I'm going to need an edge over him."

III

The Duke of Xenon's assertion had been correct—D remained blind. Robbed of his sight in his first encounter with Madame Laurencin, he now faced one fearsome opponent after another on the final day of his recovery. And the foe before the eyes he kept shut had not only been ordered to fight the Hunter for some mysterious reason; he also burned with hatred over having his beloved daughter taken from him. D had been able to destroy Dr. Gretchen because all her preening about the trap she'd laid had given him her position and allowed him to follow her movements—even as she threw the jar, she'd kept talking.

Raising the skewered D ten feet off the ground, the Duke of Xenon shook the spears in both hands with relish. A cry of pain came from D's mouth, and in addition to the lifeblood that dripped from the spearheads, the other blood that sprayed from him fell like a crimson rain.

"This isn't the way I ordinarily do things, D—but the fury of a father who's had his daughter taken is a bloody fury."

This Nobleman had always been rather cheerful in battle, but now his behavior was dismal and cruel. Skewered from the solar plexus to the neck by two spears, D appeared unable to do anything about his torment.

"But it's funny," the Duke of Xenon said, his brow crinkling inside the massive exoskeleton. "The first time I fought you, you'd already lost the use of your eyes to Madame Laurencin. However, it didn't seem like the fight of a blind man, and until this very moment I'd forgotten all about it. So, just how did you find me out, I wonder?"

"You'll see—" said a cold voice that fell on the duke from above like moonlight.

"What?"

"—soon enough."

And as he spoke, D moved. Upward? No, downward. Not even bothering to pull out the spears that ran through him, the gorgeous Hunter did completely the opposite, sliding down to the Duke of Xenon's hands as if he wished to have the weapons driven even further into him. New flesh tore, and fresh blood spurted out.

"D—damnation!" the Duke of Xenon exclaimed, but before he could let go of his spears, the sword D had raised high above his head described a mesmerizing trail of exquisite light as it sank into the head of the exoskeleton. Pale blue sparks shot out, and the night air was rocked by a cry of pain from the Duke of Xenon.

"D! Who on earth *are* you?"

Still staggering, the giant swung its massive right fist. The wind whistled. Though D blocked the blow with his left arm, the difference in their weights was so great the Hunter was knocked thirty feet, smashing against the village gates. The two long spears still jabbing through him kept him from moving his body freely.

Sparks flew from where the arc had met the Duke of Xenon's head, staining the darkness blue, but he didn't fall.

"It seems like your strike has left something to be desired, D! And now I see why. What happened to your left hand?"

D's left arm had come out of his coat—and it was cut off from the wrist down.

"Sergei, we might as well give up," Juke said, lowering his gun. "There's no point in throwing down with that monster. As long as we're still alive, there's a chance. Climb down from there."

"Sure—I'm just supposed to skulk away like some lover boy when his woman's husband comes home?" Sergei said, shrugging his shoulders as he let go of the reins.

Grand Duke Mehmet's enormous face pulled away. At that instant, Juke raised his gun with just a movement of his wrist and fired his weapon from below his waist.

The roar tore a black hole below the nose in the enormous face. Having taken the shot at close range, the gigantic puppet was left staggering.

"Yahoo!" Sergei exclaimed at the top of his lungs, slapping the reins. The horses whinnied, and the wagon sped forward, reaching sixty miles per hour in half a second.

The giant made a reflexive move for the door. Sergei aimed for his right leg. They were going to plow straight into it—but a split second before they did, he cut the wagon to the left. Its leg hit by the front right corner of the vehicle, the giant was thrown wildly off balance, landing on its left side on the floor. Encouraged by the thud it made, Sergei sped on.

"How should we get out of here?" Sergei yelled.

"Take it out the main gate," Juke shouted. His eyes were turned back toward the entrance to the warehouse. Its roof blew off. A black shape shot up, extending its arms and legs in midair.

Juke's firearm barked time and again. The stock pressed to his shoulder kicked hard enough that it should've broken the bone. The penetrator rifle D had procured could even punch through the armor plating on a flame beast. Ordinarily it would be mounted on a tripod to steady it for repeated firings, because the average person couldn't carry it around. When he'd accepted it, Juke had been completely despondent, but just now it'd saved him.

The high-caliber penetrator rounds he slammed into the giant's temple, shoulder, and side threw the attacker off balance in midair. The leap had been calculated to bring it down on the roof of the fleeing wagon, but the hands it desperately extended barely missed the edge of the vehicle, and the left half of the machine man slammed into a nearby barn. When the giant rose again, three-headed chickens, giant rabbits, and cow-pigs that had been roused from their peaceful slumber were running everywhere.

"You bastards!" the grand duke snarled, the gigantic eyes in his enormous face seeming to shoot fire. "My patience is at an end. Off to the great unknown with you!"

The machine man's mouth snapped open, and what should fly out of it but a space eater. It soared right at them.

The way it flew at precisely the same speed as them seemed a fiendish stroke meant to strike fear in Juke and his compatriot, but rather than cower, Juke raised his left hand. It almost looked as if he was stretching his arm out further than it could possibly go as he leapt up and grabbed the space eater—which had just halted over the racing wagon, formed a ring, and begun to devour itself.

Although Grand Duke Mehmet had seen it himself, he didn't really understand what had happened. Even if someone had caught it, the space eater should've bored its deadly hole through space.

When he realized nothing was happening, the grand duke started after them with earth-shaking footfalls. As he ran, he released another bug, for he'd decided that something must've been wrong with the first one. This one would perform its duty in front of the wagon. It flew far higher and faster than the last one.

But damned if Juke didn't jump up a second time. Fifteen feet he leapt to once again catch the insect in his extended left hand. And in the palm of that hand an unmistakably human mouth opened to swallow the second bug.

Once again Juke landed as beautifully on the roof as if he'd been pulled right down to it, at which point the left hand lauded him, saying, "Good job."

There could be no mistaking that hoarse voice. With an unfazed expression as it followed Juke's hand into his sleeve, it was none other than D's left hand.

On sending the two transporters into the village, where Nobility could be waiting for them anywhere, D had given them his left hand as backup. It was clear why the Duke of Xenon had finally noticed the Hunter's blindness when he fought without the use of his left hand.

"Is that the last of it?" Sergei shouted.

"Not yet," Juke replied.

The great black figure was now within sixty feet of them, and he was rapidly closing the gap.

Taking a sharp turn and crossing a bridge, they ascended a slope.

"The front door!" Sergei exclaimed on seeing the gates off in the distance.

Peeling himself from the spot where he'd been slammed into the gates, D held his sword in his teeth while he used his empty right hand to pull out the spears that skewered him. He'd probably calculated that the Duke of Xenon would have to stop attacking long enough for his exoskeleton to perform repairs, allowing D some time. Dizziness assailed him. Though part Noble, he'd lost enough blood that he should've long since died, after having been impaled and had every inch of his body burned—and he didn't have his left hand to supply him with more energy. It was surprising that he could even stand. His sword rose.

The blue light vanished from between the exoskeleton's eyes. At the same time, the duke pounced. Making a vertical leap, the exoskeleton hurled a long spear.

Tracing an elliptical path, D's blade batted it away. The Hunter's follow-up stroke should've cut the duke from one shoulder to the opposite armpit, but it met only air.

The Duke of Xenon was behind D. He'd moved with unbelievable speed.

D spun around. A third spear pierced his chest.

Landing on the ground, D was driven to one knee.

As the Duke of Xenon touched down safely, he had a new spear glowing in either hand.

Having been pierced by three spears already, D had a nearly bloodless complexion.

The Duke of Xenon raised his right hand high. The first would be a feint—the second the coup de grâce.

"This one will be through the heart."

At this point, D flowed off to the right.

Crashing through the gates, the cargo wagon appeared.

"D's compatriots?" the duke exclaimed, suddenly letting a long spear fly.

The wagon made a miraculous turn to the left, but it wasn't because of Sergei's skill at driving. He hadn't even seen the spear. But when they'd smashed blindly through the gates, there'd been an armored monstrosity right in front of them. The horses had cut to the side instinctively.

Not only were they saved, but they also reaped an unbelievable windfall. A scream rang out on the other side of the gates. What staggered into view was the enormous figure of Grand Duke Mehmet. The Duke of Xenon's spear was buried deep in his chest.

"Duke of Xenon—how could you . . ."

"Wait. This is all a terrible mistake."

While the Nobleman made a frantic apology, the gigantic Mehmet pulled the spear out of himself and hurled it back at his colleague in the exoskeleton. It pierced the Duke of Xenon through the abdomen and poked out through his back.

"Of all the stupidity—have you forgotten what we're trying to do here?" he bellowed at his colleague, but Grand Duke Mehmet kept closing on him. The machine man's mouth opened.

Just then, the giant exoskeleton began to spin like a top. For a second it kicked up dust—and then the massive form sank into the black earth.

"Taking to your heels, eh? Yes, I suppose we can't very well go about killing our own, can we?"

With nothing left to direct his rage at, the gigantic figure looked all around. The wagon was dwindling in the distance, and there was no sign of D. Presently Grand Duke Mehmet, too, vanished.

The remaining darkness was deep. Having been ordered by the mayor not to go outside, the villagers wouldn't break that prohibition until dawn, but that was a long way off, and the night was cruel and cold and choked with the reverberations of the deadly conflict.

Love and Hate from Daughter Dearest

CHAPTER 3

I

Burrowing out of the earth like an anthropomorphic drill, the Duke of Xenon reappeared some thirty minutes later at the bottom of a towering canyon about six miles north of the village—on the bank of a river, with white water splashing against the rocks right before his eyes. On throwing a switch on the interior, the super-metal-alloy armor that could bore through the hardest rock turned into a thin sheet like silver leaf, folding, curling, and doubling up until it had transformed into an ordinary bodysuit that covered the Duke of Xenon.

Though Nobles normally hated water, this man had a most atypical love of it. To be more precise, he possessed a unique physiology. Noblewomen had a distinct weakness for men who could calmly go over to water and stick their hands in. Going down to the water's edge, he plunged his right hand into the flow. The spray struck his palm, and his immortal flesh felt the same unholy chill as if he'd looked at a certain forbidden shape. Though the spray was white, he could only see its color because of his Noble's eyes, which saw as well at night as humans' eyes did at midday. Black clouds sealed off the sky as if by design, keeping any speck of light from reaching the ravine.

"Baron Balladrack's parties, boating on the river with Lord Valhalla—each and every night was filled with the moon and stars."

His voice vanished into the black surface of the water, and Roland, the Duke of Xenon, wore a terribly sentimental expression in the pitch black darkness.

"It comes as little surprise I'm a bit weary. I never suspected a young man like D existed in the world. I don't know what's become of his left hand, but if it should be reattached, I don't think I could meet him head on . . ."

He raised his right hand. A semitransparent spear formed where there had been nothing, and by the time it shot toward the opposite shore, it had taken on substance.

"Oh?" a man exclaimed with a bit of astonishment, but it was the Duke of Xenon who was in for the real surprise. The long spear he'd launched with all his might at the figure on the opposite bank of the sixty-foot-wide river had been easily caught in the person's right hand.

To be honest, the Duke of Xenon hadn't been able to make out the face of the person he was dealing with. There was no Noble save himself who'd be lurking by the water's edge at this hour, so it had to be a human, and at this time of night it could only be one of D's compatriots, so he'd launched an attack. Now, however, he could discern a regal visage.

"Baron Schuma."

"You can have this back," the Nobleman shouted, throwing the spear.

Catching the weapon aimed at his heart in one hand, the Duke of Xenon was stunned. Such speed and precision—the baron had clearly hurled it back with every intention of killing him.

"I'll be right over."

Grinning wryly at the baron's carefree cry, the Duke of Xenon turned the long spear back into suspended molecules.

The baron effortlessly crossed the swift torrent, which could have drowned even aquatic monstrosities. As proof that his feet indeed touched the water, every step he took sent white spray flying.

"Now this truly is something, Baron," the Duke of Xenon said, realizing how awkward his greeting sounded. But it was his own fault for attacking without even looking, so there wasn't much he could do about it.

"Are you okay?" the baron asked. He beamed a smile as he said it, but from the way he'd sent the spear back, he couldn't have cared less about the duke's well-being.

"Indeed. I'm one short step from running D and the others to ground," he replied, unable to conceal his anger. He hadn't liked the way the baron had asked if he was okay.

"That's splendid," the baron said, still smiling. "However, it's that last step you have to worry about."

"Why are you here?" the Duke of Xenon inquired, changing the subject. Most likely he wouldn't get along with this Nobleman, but this was their first meeting. The general had merely shown each of them holographic images of the other invited guests.

"Too bad about Dr. Gretchen, isn't it?" the baron said, and in his heart of hearts, the Duke of Xenon was taken aback. Grand Duke Mehmet himself probably didn't even know about that yet. So how did he—

"It appears that the general sees everything," the baron said. He didn't seem very impressed, though—in fact, he sounded disgusted by it. There was something in this Nobleman, with his air of fractured refinement, that made him scorn the sweeping scale of the great General Gaskell.

"What have you come here for?" the Duke of Xenon inquired, trying to rein in his irritation.

"Just out for a stroll," the baron answered, breaking into a grin. "Or so I'd like to tell you, but the truth is, there's a spot in this area that interests me."

"Oh?" the Duke of Xenon replied. He wished to part company with this man so badly it was killing him.

"There's a waterfall up ahead. You could probably already tell from the sound of the water splashing. Behind the cataract, the lowly humans used to keep a lair. The odious place was cleaned out long ago, melted away to nothing, and the person in charge of all that was my very own uncle."

"Fascinating."

"So this evening, with the general's permission, I set out to inspect the historic ruins my family had the honor of destroying. Would you care to join me?"

"I'm sorry, but I must decline."

"That's most regrettable. Well then, I shall see you again soon."

And saying this, the baron headed off along the shore toward the roar of the falls, only to turn again after five or six steps and say, "Kindly hurry back to the castle. My instincts are telling me D is close by."

And with that he walked off.

"What's that idiot talking about?" the Duke of Xenon grumbled, spitting up the black wad of sediment that had gelled in his belly. The form of Baron Schuma had already melted into the darkness. Now disgusted beyond words, the Duke of Xenon kicked a stone from the riverbank into the flow. The noise of the river swallowed the sound.

Suddenly the Duke of Xenon looked up; he'd heard a different noise. It was definitely artificial—a wagon speeding in the night air.

"It can't be—they're here?"

In amazement, he turned his face in the direction from which the sound was coming—and donned an intense expression of delight when he saw the sheer rock cliff.

"If the wagon's coming here, then D will come, too. This time, I'll do away with the lot of them."

The silvery membrane wrapped around his body. As the river voiced its endless laughter, the armored combatant stood on its bank. In his right hand a spear instantly appeared. And in a single bound he crossed the same river Baron Schuma had walked across, going headfirst toward the sheer cliff, then spinning like a top to bore into it.

Radar within the exoskeleton had already put onscreen a graphic representation of the size, shape, and mass of what ran across the ground—it was definitely that cargo wagon. Was D there, too? Even if he wasn't, the duke could always capture the others to lure the Hunter out. No, that would be too much trouble. He'd kill them. If he did that, the Hunter would undoubtedly succumb to his anger and come looking for a fight.

Although he was sadly mistaken on both counts, the Duke of Xenon believed these things anyway.

Traveling at full speed, he began his ascent.

Three hundred feet shy of the slope into the gorge, Sergei cut to the left and drove into the forest. He and Juke set about camouflaging their vehicle, covering it with leaves and branches they'd prepared ahead of time.

"The villagers won't come after us at this hour, so we're safe there, but the Nobility are a threat. If they were to use wind devils, they could find us, no problem," Sergei grumbled.

"Settle down. Now hurry up and go tell them down below."

"Yes, sir."

Once they'd finished, Sergei took one of the flares from the front seat and headed into the forest—he still had on a pair of infrared goggles that allowed him to see in the dark. Taking the descending road, he was buffeted by the night wind as he stood at the top of the cliff, looking down at the waterfall. Dawn was beginning to spread in the eastern sky. The night was at an end.

He was approaching a terrific splashing sound. Halting, he found the river running right by him. His field of view was dyed green by his infrared goggles. The band of water dropped in a waterfall about a hundred feet to Sergei's right. Directly below him were Gordo and the others.

Holding the flare at an angle so it would fall into the waterfall's basin, Sergei pulled the cord on its bottom end. A pink ball of light lent the same hue to its smoky tail as the base of the waterfall swallowed it. Even behind the wall of water, there was no way they could miss that light. Gordo would be making preparations to leave while they headed down for him. Those preparations, however, merely meant telling one of the two women what was happening.

"Damn, that Schuma's a lucky bastard!" a voice called out behind the transporter, and it was one he'd heard before. As his right hand reached for his shirt pocket, his whole body froze. Three thousand volts of current had just shot through Sergei.

"Y-y-y-you—"

He'd intended to call the Noble a son of a bitch, but his tongue didn't get that far.

"Where is Lady Ann? No, you don't have to answer that. She's behind the falls. My compatriot's already gone back there. As for you—would you rather be a corpse or a hostage?"

"Y-y-y-you—"

"Have it your way. As long as the fellow in the woods remains, you're just excess baggage. Die, then."

The fingertip the Duke of Xenon laid on Sergei's shoulder was about to send ten thousand volts of current through the man when a voice on the dawn breeze called out, "Father!"

The Duke of Xenon was so surprised, he took his hand away from his foe's shoulder, and Sergei collapsed on the spot.

Up ahead and to the left, Lady Ann stood with her feet together on a boulder that jutted at an angle from the ground. Her legs were together so tightly, there wasn't room to slip a piece of paper between them.

"Oh, Lady Ann—" the Duke of Xenon began before breaking off, about to say something about her being okay but finishing before anyone ever heard those words.

"Father—do you still pursue these people?" the girl said in response, but in her voice there wasn't a trace of the emotion expected from a daughter being reunited with her own father.

"I have no business with them. D's the only one I want."

"Still you persist?"

"Are you out to become a traitor, Lady Ann? The great General Gaskell will never forgive you."

"I'll pay a call on him later to offer my apologies."

"And you think the general will accept that?"

"Then I shall have to kill him."

His beloved daughter said this so impassively that the Duke of Xenon could only stare at her in amazement.

"Just as I thought—love for D has addled your brains. Lady Ann, come back with me. I'll free you from this brainwashing. But before we go, put this on."

The Duke of Xenon extended his right hand. In it he held a small atomizer. It sprayed a mist that enveloped the girl's body.

"Today's the third day. Your shields have worn out. This will give you another three days," he said in a gentle tone, but Lady Ann looked melancholy.

"Please, forget about me for good. The girl you see before you isn't the Lady Ann you loved, Father."

"Oh, how can you say that?" the Duke of Xenon said, extending both of his huge hands as if in appeal. A second later, purple light connected Lady Ann and the Duke of Xenon's right index finger.

"Aaaah!"

Up on the boulder, Lady Ann bent back as far as she possibly could. It looked as if she had been completely paralyzed, and white smoke rose from her body.

In the Duke of Xenon's eyes lurked madness deeper than the darkness.

"If I have to hand you over to another, I'd sooner—no, just consider this your punishment for betraying your father and abandoning him. Die here and now!"

But these shouts of sorrow and insanity, heard only by the night, stopped there. As if he'd suddenly recalled something, he immediately said in a vacant tone, "Wait. Wait just a minute . . . You're . . . Yes, I'm sure . . ."

If he'd had another second, the next thing he said surely would've explained everything. However, the eyes of the Duke of Xenon's exoskeleton glowed red as he turned to his right, and the road.

Lady Ann collapsed, just as Sergei had.

The figure who stood about fifteen feet away, with watery light behind him, looked like a grim reaper in black who'd just arrived on his trusty steed to oversee the demise of the other players. However, this grim reaper was beautiful. So beautiful you could call him the devil. So beautiful he might be mistaken for an angel. But before she could do either, a person would undoubtedly offer up her life and soul in rapture.

D.

II

"Do you have any idea how I've searched for you?" the Duke of Xenon said in a monotone, as if reading the words off a card. "Oh, you don't have your left hand back yet, do you? Great! That means the battle's as good as decided."

"You didn't have to search for me," came the response in a shadowy tone that was somehow crystal clear at the same time. D was on horseback. "I've been following you all along. And now I've finally caught up to you."

"What?" The Duke of Xenon was perplexed, but then a certain memory flashed in his brain like lightning: *My instincts are telling me D is close by.*

"For how long?"

"Ever since you disappeared in front of the gate. The sound of you burrowing through the earth reaches the surface fairly well," D said, but anyone without the duke's ears probably wouldn't have heard it. The reason it'd taken D so long to catch up to the Duke of Xenon in the flesh was because the armored exoskeleton could travel in a straight line underground, while the Hunter's cyborg horse had been forced to blaze a trail through the woods.

"I'm surprised you had the nerve to follow me, especially wounded like that. And without your left hand to cover for those wounds, you think you can defeat me—Roland, the Duke of Xenon? On top of all that, aren't you still blind, D?"

D had both eyes shut firmly.

"Don't do it . . . D . . . You mustn't . . . fight Father . . ." Lady Ann groaned, her words creeping across the ground like the speech of the dead.

The figure of D, covered in blood after having been run through with three of the Duke of Xenon's long spears, was reflected in her eyes. Tears glistened in those eyes, which could only be described as large and round. It wasn't that she was moved by the ferocious spirit he displayed in pursuing his foe in his condition, and now preparing to cross swords again; she wept at the sight of the man she loved covered in blood. She didn't care about her father, or the cargo wagon, or the great General Gaskell. Her tears were an unvoiced plea, from her to him, to not do battle in this condition but to flee from this place as soon as possible.

But the man she loved didn't demonstrate so much as a mote of understanding of her feelings. D drew his sword. His body went into motion.

Astonished, the Duke of Xenon backed away. Neither the speed of the Hunter's leap nor the aura that crashed down on him like the angry sea seemed that of a dying man. The Duke of Xenon parried the sword the young man brought down with his long spear, which broke in two. Tendrils of blue electromagnetism reached out from the right shoulder of his armor like spidery limbs. Another fraction of an inch and D's blade probably would've reached the duke's body within.

Groaning, the Duke of Xenon watched D land, and then circled his armored form around behind the Hunter. His speed was in excess of Mach 3. The Duke of Xenon had plenty of time to take aim at D's back.

Was this to be a replay of the battle in front of the main gate?

A flash of light came from D. He'd reversed his grip on his sword and made a thrust behind him. The blade penetrated the armor like it was paper, piercing the Duke of Xenon through the heart.

"Aaaah!"

Scattering howls of pain and curses, the Duke of Xenon once again raised a long spear, and then brought it down. It was easily deflected.

There was another flash from D.

The massive exoskeleton became thin shreds of paper dancing in the wind. All that remained on the ground was an imposing man struggling to retain his footing. He took a step toward Lady Ann, who was now sitting up. His body started to separate just above the hip. When he fell, a startling amount of black blood spurted out, shrouding the two halves of his body like a fog.

"Ann . . . Lady Ann . . ." the Duke of Xenon called out to his daughter, the thread-thin voice dribbling out of him with the black blood.

Lady Ann crawled over to him.

"I am destroyed. Stay with me . . . Ann."

"Very well, Father."

After a desperate effort to pull herself up, Lady Ann laid her father's head on her lap and gently stroked his hair.

"Ann . . . My Ann."

"Father," the girl whispered. There was a hint of loneliness in her blue eyes.

"What is it, Ann?"

"It's not good to die with a lie on your lips. Call me by the name of the one you really love—Mother's name," the girl whispered. Now there was a hint of hatred in her blue eyes.

"What are you . . . talking about? Ann . . . I loved . . . only you."

"Liar."

Ann opened her mouth. And then a crimson flower blossomed on the Duke of Xenon's forehead.

"A-Ann?"

"This is your punishment for lying."

A horrible look of pain hung on the duke's face. The deadly blossom was sucking the last bit of life from him. In the darkened region devoid of light, the flower began to take on a mysterious red glow.

"Your hour is at hand, Father—speak the truth. Say the name you called me when you violated me."

The Duke of Xenon's lips pulled up at the corners. One last spasm assailed his flesh. His last breath escaped, accompanied by a hoarse voice. "Ann . . ."

Taking her gaze from her father, who was turning to dust, Lady Ann rose unsteadily to her feet. Fixing her eyes on an empty spot in space, she said, "A liar to the very end . . . You may be at peace now, but I won't know salvation for all eternity."

A single tear fell from her eye. Did she fail to wipe it away because she wanted D to see it?

Turning to the young man in black, she asked, "Could you see when you stabbed behind you at Father?"

D's eyes were open, reflecting the darkness. Three days had passed since Madame Laurencin had taken his vision with her poison. And the moment Lady Ann asked about it was exactly when it had returned.

"Hey! Sergei!" they heard Juke cry, his footsteps audible in the distance. Before long his form came into view.

"Oh, is this where you've been?" he said, and as he watched his fellow transporter cling to D's shoulder to get to his feet, a look of relief crossed his face for a moment. Then, with a flash of realization, he said, "You should probably take this."

Taking the left hand out of his coat pocket, he gave it back to D. When D placed it against the wound on his left wrist, the seam vanished, and D was once again in possession of two hands.

After Sergei finished explaining the situation to Juke, the group's attention inevitably shifted to Lady Ann.

"Why are you here? What about Gordo?" asked Juke.

"He's asleep down in that cavern."

"You did something to him, didn't you?"

"Aren't you the suspicious one! Although in this case, you're correct."

"You were trying to escape, eh?"

"I intended to go to D. When I got to the top of the cliff, Father emerged from the ground."

"He said something funny," Sergei said, his tongue still numb. "Something about his compatriot already going behind the waterfall. Wait! There was something else . . . He mentioned Schuma being the lucky one."

The figure in black walked past the rest of the group.

"D?"

"Get ready to set off," D said as he moved toward the edge of the cliff.

"I'm going, too!"

The instant Lady Ann started to run toward him, his black raiment became one with the darkness. And just shortly thereafter, so did the blond girl.

After seeing the two of them throw themselves from the precipice, Sergei and Juke looked at each other, then headed back the way they'd come.

When D entered the cavern behind the waterfall, Baron Schuma was sitting cross-legged near where Gordo and Rosaria lay.

"Long time no see, D," he called out without turning.

D had made no attempt to muffle his footsteps or hide his presence.

"I'm fortunate. Imagine running into you without making any effort at all! Just so you know, I hold the lives of these two in my hand. Not even your sword could finish me fast enough."

"What have you come here for?" D inquired.

There were no bite marks on Gordo's or Rosaria's necks. But a Noble who could have two sleeping humans before him and do nothing was to be feared all the more.

"A look around this cave. It used to house the remains of a human religious center, but my uncle got rid of them. In fact, he did such a thorough job that I'm frightened in spite of myself."

"Get up."

"Have a seat," the baron said, slapping the ground to his left. "There's actually something that interests me. Until I get it squared away, I won't feel much like fighting you."

"And what would that be?" asked a voice that wasn't D's.

The baron turned, startled, and stared at D's left hand. "Oh, I see. So that's it," he said with a nod. "Well, you seem more urbane than your owner. What I'd like to discuss is this: Why were we summoned?"

"Wasn't it to be assassins for General Gaskell?" the hoarse voice responded. Its tone seemed to question the need to state the obvious.

"I understand that. But there's something strange about him, too."

"You don't say. What would that be?"

"The fact that he doesn't know why he selected us," the baron said quite plainly. But there was a clear ring of distress to his voice. "What's more, I'd like to know why we were brought back to life. No—there's another question behind that one. To wit, for what purpose was General Gaskell resurrected?"

"To slay D, probably."

"Why?"

"That's what we'd like to know," the left hand remarked in disgust.

Baron Schuma fell silent. The only noise was that of the waterfall. The electronic light Gordo had set up made the group's long shadows dance on the distant rock walls. The light of dawn hadn't reached into the cavern yet.

Before long, the baron spoke again, saying, "General Gaskell and the rest of us entered a lengthy sleep. That's the problem—none of us was destroyed. As punishment, all of us were condemned to sleep for all eternity, by command of the Sacred Ancestor. In other words, some might say we were put to sleep to await this day."

"Hmm."

"D!" the baron called out, his tone changing. It echoed off the rocky walls in all its awful gravity. "You must tell me. Why are we after you?"

There was no reply.

"Why would anyone send us after you?"

Still no reply.

"And something else, D. I have been forced to come to a chilling conclusion. This is why I really must have you make one thing clear for me: Who are you, D?"

The electronic flames played intermittent shadows and light across handsome features that didn't seem to be of this world.

III

"You're not going to answer me, are you?" the baron said, extending both arms and stretching his back. "To be honest, I'm afraid to hear the reply. I've never felt this way before. The stench of blood wafts from your body—the Duke of Xenon's been destroyed, hasn't he?"

The figure in vermilion stood up.

"In which case, it's my turn next. But before we do that, there's something I'd like to look into."

Rapping his walking stick against his shoulder, the baron proceeded into the depths of the cavern. Looking back, he turned his gaze to Gordo and Rosaria and said, "Though I've moved away, the two of them remain in just as much danger. Wait until I've attended to my business."

Though there seemed to be something placid about the man, D knew the power that lay within him.

Halting before the furthest rock wall, where the light didn't even reach, the baron rapped on it with his stick.

"Ah! There's an X mark. Uncle always was a philistine. If he had to leave a mark, he could've made it something a little more difficult for people to recognize. Apparently, he buried something here."

"What's that?" D's left hand inquired.

"According to family legends, a certain weapon."

"A weapon?"

"Uncle oversaw the training of elite combat personnel and the development of weapons at the Sacred Ancestor's palace. He was a man blessed with a great sense of humor. Thanks to this, it suddenly occurred to him as he was working under the Sacred Ancestor that he should create something utterly preposterous. In other words, he invented a weapon to destroy the Sacred Ancestor."

For a moment, another sound dominated the cavern, where the roar of the cataract alone had held sway: a sound known as silence.

Then, the hoarse voice said with appreciable amusement, "You've got a twisted family."

"Had he shown it to his acquaintances, I suppose he would've been considered an impressive man, but he was actually rather timid. After creating it, my uncle grew afraid. However, he didn't have the courage to destroy his creation. He thought about a place to hide it but quickly grew uneasy, having the feeling that wherever he concealed it, he couldn't keep it safe from the eyes of the Sacred Ancestor. Then, after giving up drinking even the blood wine from Efferis, he came up with the perfect hiding place. After melting the ancient human ruins, he used the very same location to conceal the proof of his treachery born of an outlandish joke—quite an inspiration, wouldn't you say?"

His walking stick came down on the little mark. Cracks raced out in all directions, and a hole the size of a grown man's head opened.

"Don't move, D. Stay right where you are," the baron said in a friendly tone as he shifted his stick to his left hand and thrust his right into the hole.

"Eh?" he exclaimed, tilting his head to one side and knitting his brow at a strange sound on the other side of the hole—that of something being caught and torn.

"Ow!" he groaned, pulling his arm back out. But the limb he extracted was cut off at the elbow.

"It should've been enough to simply bury the weapon. He really was quite perverse," the baron cursed, roughly thrusting the stick he held in his left hand into the hole. A scream rang out, but it was quickly silenced.

The baron stuck his right arm in and pulled it out again. From the elbow down it was back to normal. But then, that's why he was an immortal Noble.

Inserting his hand into the hole once again, he strained to twist his face in D's direction as he said, "It's in there. Now, what do you think I intend to do with it?"

The Nobleman broke into a grin.

"I'll use it on you, of course. My uncle left papers detailing its power and usage. It should be more than enough to slay the likes of you. So, how about it? Are you willing to sacrifice the lives of those two humans to resist me?"

"He's probably bluffing," said the hoarse voice.

"Do you have the nerve to try me?" the baron sneered, looking at the Hunter's left hand. "No, the man they call D probably has courage enough to fill the seven seas. But I see that one of those humans has hired you as a guard. Would you stoop so low as to sacrifice your employer?"

This was obviously the greatest crisis that D had encountered. No one spoke with reverence of a man who would allow others to die for him. And the weapon that would be directed at this young man wasn't the sort of thing he could shrug off.

The baron declared, "In that case, have at you, D. What you do next will show me what kind of man you are."

The baron started to pull his arm out, and at that very moment a crimson rose opened on top of his head. Its lovely appearance aside, the blossom delivered hellish torment to his immortal flesh. Wailing as he reached for the flower, the baron reeled backward.

"Who—who's done this?"

A second flower blossomed right in the middle of his pale, sweaty brow. Letting out another shriek, he writhed as he pulled out his right hand. It didn't hold anything.

Turning, his hate-filled eyes caught a figure at the entrance to the cavern, far behind D—a diminutive figure who stood dripping wet. It was Lady Ann. She was soaked because, when jumping down from the cliff with D, she alone had landed in the pool at the bottom. Naturally, there was no reason why D would've helped her back out. Reaching shore on her own, she'd dragged herself inside. And that was when she saw Baron Schuma menacing D.

Obsessed as she was, Lady Ann viewed any foe of D's as a foe of hers. She didn't care what happened to Gordo or Rosaria. She sent her deadly blooms sailing toward one of her father's compatriots—a man boasting of triumph over the man she loved.

"Now, D!" she said, but D had already sprung, and was bringing his longsword down on the baron's head.

The baron didn't have time to raise his stick to ward off the blow.

But in that deadly instant, the rock wall exploded. Even D was caught off guard by this, his body pelted with pieces of stone and a gust from the blast throwing him to the center of the cavern.

"D?" Lady Ann cried out as she raced toward him. As she did so, she saw the strange thing that appeared where the rock wall had been.

At first glance, it appeared to be a reddish black mass about six and a half feet in diameter. Wrinkles and creases ran through it in some areas, while others swelled like balloons. Even more bizarre were the four-inch-long barbs that protruded from every inch of it, then pulled back in, extending and retracting over and over, so the essentially spherical shape didn't seem the least bit stable.

"D—what is this?" asked Lady Ann.

"Gotta be the weapon's guardian," the hoarse voice replied, but the moment it did so, one of the barbs on the sphere shot out at D like a whip. When he deflected it with his sword, a second barb assailed him, then a third. Fending all of them off, D dashed between the unprepared whips toward the creature's body. His blade pierced it without a sound.

After pulling the sword he'd buried to the hilt halfway out again, D leapt back. A yellowish ichor that had apparently come from the creature's body clung to the blade, and thanks to it, the sword had begun to melt and give off white smoke. Putting his left hand against the blade, D pulled the sword out all the way to the tip. The melting stopped.

The liquid was a powerful acid. It'd spilled from the wound D's sword had caused, turning the already melted rock into boiling-hot mud as it began to dissolve.

"This is what melted those ancient ruins—run for it!" the hoarse voice cried, but there was no point listening to it. White smoke already filled the cavern, and the floor and ceiling were both collapsing.

Looking back as he ran toward the cataract with Gordo under one arm and Rosaria under the other, D saw, in the far reaches of the white smoke, the silhouette of the deflating globe spilling deadly fluid everywhere.

"Is it clear whether Schuma is alive or dead?" the great General Gaskell asked, his voice issuing from somewhere in the darkness. His tone suggested neither sorrow nor regret. "Madame Laurencin, Dr. Gretchen, and the Duke of Xenon have all been slain, and although Grand Duke Mehmet hasn't, his wounds keep him occupied. Including you, only four of the resurrected remain. What's more, one of the four has sided with the enemy. I have to wonder if any of you will actually do any good."

"I resent that, General," said another voice. It was that of the Dark One—Major General Gillis. "However, there certainly may be something to what you say. I have faced him myself. What I can tell you about D's ability wouldn't help us at all. But if I may, I'd like to ask you this—just who *is* D?"

"I don't know," Gaskell answered simply. "There wasn't a single mention of him in the data I was given by the Sacred Ancestor.

And it's pointless to speculate why that might be. All we can do is slay the bastard."

"Indeed, milord. However, the only problem is that those you've summoned might not be up to the task."

Gaskell donned a bitter grin. He had no choice but to nod in agreement.

"However, I have a proposal for you."

"What would that be?" the great general asked, his gaze flying up toward the unseen ceiling.

"Combining the lives of Schuma, Mehmet, and Lady Ann, you might invite one more. That should certainly be possible."

If Major General Gillis was expecting a refusal, he was to be sadly disappointed. The great General Gaskell allowed himself to sink into a silence heavier than the darkness.

"Was I out of place to suggest such a thing?" Major General Gillis inquired apprehensively after some time had passed.

"We're one short," the general responded gravely, freezing the other Nobleman. "With four lives instead of three, I might select a worthy replacement. Oh, that's merely a jest. But this will definitely call for three lives."

"Of course, *milord*," Major General Gillis said; apparently he was quite the flatterer.

"I have orders for you, Major General Gillis."

"Yes, sir."

"Devote every ounce of your energies toward defeating D. That is my condition if you don't wish to be added as the fourth life."

"It will be my pleasure."

"It would seem to be too much of a task for you alone. Take some of my chamberlains with you. *These* are the locations of Schuma and Mehmet."

While it was unclear how he shared that information with the Nobleman, a startled cry of "Oh!" rang out in the darkness.

"It shall be done. Milord, you may begin preparations to awaken your newest guest." Gillis then continued, "Actually, I've had a secret love for the daughter of Roland, the Duke of Xenon. Now I might have contact with her openly."

First his ebullient tone and then the rest of his presence vanished. As he disappeared, the southern Frontier's greatest warrior, guardian, and overseer, General Gaskell, spat, "Filthy little pedophile."

The Plague Village

CHAPTER 4

I

"What's this? A roadblock?" Juke said from the driver's seat, seeing men on the road about sixty feet ahead.

The men were most definitely armed, and there was a barricade behind them, made of wood and wire fencing, that crossed the road.

The group had left the waterfall behind them, and it was now late in the afternoon. The road they were on would bring them to their next destination—the village of Hardue—in about twenty minutes.

The sky bore clouds even heavier than those of the day before. Not a beam of sunlight deigned to grace the road.

Once the transporters had stopped about thirty feet away, two of the five men came over to them. They carried pneumatic guns pointed toward the sky. Of course, if the situation called for it, they were ready to point them at the group and open fire in a heartbeat, so it hardly proved them harmless. Bandit groups would use every trick in the book.

The men gave the names of two different villages about twenty miles south and told them the reason the road had been blockaded.

"An epidemic?"

"Yep. It's the fountain plague."

Both Juke and Gordo, who was on the roof, were speechless.

It was one of the worst diseases of all the contagions on the Frontier, and it'd wiped out more villages than anyone could count. Whenever even a single person came down with it, surrounding villages would join forces to seal off the infected village and wait for the disease to pass. In most cases, that would be when the entire population had died out.

"If it's fountain plague, we can fix them," Juke said, but his words only put a grimmer look in the men's eyes. "Seriously. See, a hospital in the Capital has developed a special medicine for it. And we're scheduled to deliver it to Hardue. They're signed up for any new medicines."

What villages on the Frontier needed more than anything was new drugs from the Capital. Ageless and immortal, the Nobility weren't particularly intent on developing new medical treatments for themselves, but for the humans on whom they subsisted, they used their scientific prowess to develop drugs and build hospitals. It was something like the love an owner shows for his pet dog, only a bit more twisted. Even after the Nobility had vanished into obscurity, humans were left to run the medical facilities they'd left behind, and though they couldn't comprehend some of the equipment or the theories behind it, they somehow managed to produce results. Frontier villages that were especially rich made arrangements with transport services like Juke's so that new drugs and medical equipment would be delivered as soon as they were developed, no questions asked. And the village of Hardue was one such place.

"We can't trust these guys," one of the men said to the other in a doubtful tone. Tension raced through the group by the barricade. "Fountain plague breaks out in the village, and the very next day someone comes along with a special medicine for it. It's all a little too neat."

"What would we stand to gain by lying? If the symptoms showed up yesterday, there's still time to treat them. The victims could get better."

"And what happens if they don't get better?" the other man asked. "What are you gonna do if all of *you* come down with it, too? We don't want any more trouble than we've already got here. So either turn back or take a detour."

"Don't you get it? We've got medicine. If we inject them with this, it'll cure them of the fountain plague."

The two men looked at each other. With a despicable smile on his face, the first one to address them said, "And if that special medicine doesn't work, we'll have to keep you locked in Hardue. But there's no way we could stop this big ol' wagon of yours from busting through our barricade. We couldn't have you bringing any more weapons into Hardue with you, either. Leave your wagon here and go in unarmed, and we'll allow it."

"That's complete bullshit!" Juke said, his eyes bulging. "It'd take another twenty minutes to reach Hardue in this wagon. On foot, that'd be six hours. You think we could spend that long walking a road crawling with monsters without a single weapon?"

"In that case, we can't let you go."

The two men took a step back, and the group at the barricade leveled their guns at the transporters. At the same time, Sergei was up on the roof taking aim at the two men with a gunpowder firearm.

Grinning thinly, the second man pointed toward the barricade and said, "Give it a rest. That thing over there's a portable missile launcher. Seems folks in the Capital call it 'Rodan.' You can shoot us, but that wagon of yours will get blown to smithereens. That the sort of thing a transporter would want?"

A pained expression stole onto Juke's face. A transporter's cargo was as important as his life or his honor.

The two men laughed mockingly, and then one of them said, "Now, about the toll—what do you say we make it half your merchandise?"

A shadow fell across the men, for another figure had come into view—the shadowy form of a guard who'd been behind the wagon and out of their sight until now.

"D," Juke murmured.

"D?"

Whatever that name called to mind, the pair looked up at the rider with fear on their faces as the figure in black grabbed them both by the collar and lifted them into the air, before they could say another word. Even Juke and the other transporters found it strange how the two men were as motionless as corpses.

"Stop it. We'll do whatever you say!" said one.

"Please don't kill us," the other pleaded feebly. They seemed quite terrified of D.

"Set the two of them down!" a man at the barricade shouted, one hand cupped by the side of his mouth. To his left, "Rodan" was taking aim. Its base was huge, but the tube housing its black missile was long and thin.

"What do you want to do?" D asked Juke.

"Go, of course. That's our job."

"Stick with me," D told them, and then he started to ride toward the barricade.

The men manning it were shaken as well. D and his compatriots were traveling in the path of their missile. But what disturbed them more than anything was the beauty of the young rider. It was unearthly.

"Halt!" someone shouted. "Halt. If you don't, we'll blow you away!"

But they knew they couldn't. He was too close, and one of those missiles cost as much as fifty head of cattle; they couldn't very well use it to settle their own personal quarrels.

The air whistled, and the person manning the launcher felt a slight tremor coming down the tube that discharged the missile.

D returned his blade to its sheath.

The men stood stock still and forgot all about shooting them, probably robbed of their souls more by D's looks than by his unearthly air. D passed them without uttering a word. He was followed by the wagon carrying Juke and Gordo, both of whom were grinning as if to say, *This time, it's our turn to laugh.*

As they started to disappear down the road, someone far behind them growled, "Dirty bastards!"

But when the missile was brought to bear on the transport party, the man on the launcher learned what that earlier tremor had been. The front half of the firing tube had just fallen to the ground noisily. The tube was made of an alloy that was said to be able to withstand a one-ton impact. In the faint gloom, the piece rolling across the ground showed a nice, smooth cut.

As they approached the entrance to the village, the pair of men the Hunter held up in the air began to display a different kind of fear.

"Please, just set us down already. If we get any closer, we'll get infected!"

"For the love of heaven, spare us, please. I don't wanna catch the stinkin' fountain plague!"

The two men moved their arms and legs frantically. Even though D was holding up around three hundred fifty pounds with that one arm, it didn't move in the least.

But even Juke seemed to feel sorry for the pair, saying, "You can let 'em go now."

"They'll just do the same thing again," D replied, silencing the transporter. After all, these men had demanded half their merchandise. "They've probably made similar demands of those trying to get out of the village. That way, they could just take their money and finish them off."

Judging from the way the pair stopped struggling and averted their gazes, the Hunter's remarks were probably right on the mark.

"You sons of bitches . . . You didn't!" Gordo groaned angrily up on the roof, but just then Juke's form tensed in the driver's seat.

"Someone's coming!" he cried, pointing straight ahead.

About a hundred feet away, a couple had appeared where the road detoured to the right: a boy and girl who looked to be around ten years old. They seemed to be a couple because the hands at the

end of their wire-thin arms were clasped. For some reason, they were as red as if they'd been brushed with paint from the tops of their heads to the tips of their sandaled toes.

The pair the Hunter held aloft screamed.

"It's the fountain plague," said Juke. "Sergei, get that medicine ready."

Halting the wagon, Juke climbed down from the driver's seat. Along with Sergei, who came out of the vehicle carrying a paper parcel, he hurried over to the boy and girl. However, before they got to them, the two youthful figures fell to the ground.

On reaching them, Juke and Sergei held their breath and froze in their tracks. Neither of them had ever seen a victim of fountain plague in the flesh before.

The boy and girl were both covered with blood, but they weren't injured. The men knew that. Even now, fresh blood continued to ooze from the children's faces, necks, arms, and legs. It came from every pore in their bodies.

According to *The Complete Book of Frontier Medicine*, which was distributed to every village on the Frontier, this strain of bacteria was carried by an as-yet unidentified species of supernatural beast, and when it infected humans, they would experience intense vertigo, malaise, and fatigue. What's more, within three hours they would begin to bleed from their pores starting in the area near the lungs, and if no effective steps were taken to treat them, they would be dead within twelve hours after the bleeding started. Although the immediate cause of death was blood loss, the process by which the bacteria inside the body caused this reaction was still being investigated, and no effective treatment had been discovered. The sight of an infected person staggering around covered with blood was chilling, and the relentless manner in which the lifeblood pumped from her body led to the sickness being dubbed "fountain plague."

Though the sight was so horrible it had made the transporters stop in spite of themselves, their human emotions soon returned to them. Tearing open the package, Sergei took out a pair of painless disposable syringes loaded with medicine and handed one of them to Juke. The drug was injected directly into a vein. The children were so emaciated there was no trouble locating a vein, so that part was easy enough.

"I wonder if we're in time?" Sergei inquired, a grave look on his face, but Juke could only tilt his head to one side with an even graver expression. It certainly looked like they were too late.

The boy and girl had fallen still holding hands, and their eyes opened simultaneously.

"Holy!" Sergei whooped with joy.

"Get ready to do a transfusion," Juke ordered him before leaning over the children to ask, "Are you in pain?"

"Yeah." The boy probably lacked even the strength to lie. He inquired feebly, "What about Ann?"

Juke replied gently, "She's right beside you. Holding your hand."

"Good. I didn't want her to go alone. I'll go right along with her."

"Don't talk. You'll feel better soon."

But once he'd said that, Juke realized the gravity of the situation, and he made a wretched face.

"I'm glad. This sickness really, really hurts."

"I know. You've held up so well," Juke said, taking his hand and wiping the boy's red face. There was a chance of catching it through epidermal contact, but that didn't bother him. The skin that appeared had a waxy hue.

"Mister . . . have you got medicine with you? Can you cure this?"

"Yeah."

"Then . . . save everyone in the village."

Juke suddenly looked next to the boy—at the girl.

"My father . . . and my mother are suffering . . . The two of us . . . came to get help," she continued. "But . . . those men shot at us . . ."

The two men averted their eyes from Juke and Sergei.

"She—she's lying!"

"They're horrible!" the girl said. Her cute little face was stained red up to her hair. "They told us to go get money . . . from the villagers. Said they'd let us go if we did. But all they did . . . was take the money . . ."

"You fucking bastards," Sergei said, rising to his feet.

He drew his gun. Pressing it against the forehead of one, then the other, he said, "I know you couldn't let them out. But stealing money from them when they're just trying to buy their own survival is something even the damned Nobility wouldn't stoop to!"

And while he was saying that, the emotion within him grew stronger and stronger, until he was ready to explode.

"Die!"

A second later, the pair vanished from in front of his quaking gun barrel. D had hoisted them up.

"Stay out of this!" the transporter told him.

"These two will get the death they deserve," the Hunter replied in a voice that called to mind the stillness of a wintry night, and it chilled not only the pair, but Sergei as well.

"That's right," Juke said in a low tone. "Right now I don't feel like seeing any more death. These two kids just passed on."

II

Sergei's shoulders drooped, and he gazed down at the red faces of the dead.

"You know, it kinda looks like they're smiling."

"They probably felt relieved because they ran into us. Even if I wind up going to hell, that's bound to make my punishment a little lighter," Juke said, gently stroking the cheeks of the two children.

"Shouldn't we bury them?"

"Later. Let's get the medicine to the village."

"Okay." Putting his gun away, Sergei spat at the two men, then went back to the children and folded his hands.

A beautiful shadow fell beside him.

"D?"

Setting the two men he held down on the ground, the gorgeous Hunter pushed their faces toward the innocent faces of the dead. Although the men kicked against the ground and tried to flee, his iron grip would never allow them to escape.

"Stop it!"

"Help! You'll get us infected."

Their pleas gave way to screams as he pressed the men's lips against the cheeks of the boy and the girl, as if to kiss them goodbye.

The pair collapsed on the spot—D's spell over them had finally broken. They didn't move a muscle. They'd fainted.

"They got what they deserved . . . but you can still be pretty harsh," Juke said as he gave D a fearful look. "They've lost their minds! Of course, where the Frontier's concerned, that's probably all for the best."

As he was about to walk back to the wagon, he gasped and stopped in his tracks. In front of him stood the other girl named Ann.

"He said her name was Ann, didn't he?"

Eyes as sharp and clear as glass reflected the face of the girl on the ground.

"Yeah, he did."

"Why do human beings die? From sicknesses and things like that, I mean."

"Because we're human!" Juke answered.

"Hmm. Are you crying?"

"I suppose I am."

"But you *know* human beings die, don't you?"

"Yeah."

"Then why does this sadden you? It's the natural outcome."

"I'll murder you, you little monster!" Sergei shouted in the distance.

"Knock it off," Juke told him, and then he said to Lady Ann, "Don't you feel anything at all about that other Ann dying?"

"Not a thing."

Juke nodded. His expression suggested he'd just confirmed something.

"Good enough. Now, get back to the wagon. We're going into the village."

At just about the same time that D and his group were having their confrontation at the blockade, Grand Duke Mehmet was in the northern forest. An enormous figure leaned against a tremendous languia tree that looked to be thirty feet in diameter, while beside that figure there was a second that looked exactly like it but smaller—a normal, human-sized figure that was also the grand duke. Now his actual form and his surrogate were finally face to face. The strange thing was, when the real grand duke put his hands behind his head, the oversized impostor struck the same pose.

"That D is a monster," said the Noble, who, from the human perspective, was considered nothing short of a monster himself. "I saw the Duke of Xenon's remains. Dr. Gretchen, too, has been destroyed. It doesn't seem there's a chance in the world of me triumphing over him all alone. I think perhaps it would be best if I made a stealthy retreat from the front lines."

Taking his hands from behind his head, he ran them over his upper body.

"I was cut here . . . here . . . and here," he said, staring at the same spots on his gigantic doppelgänger.

As long as his true form was unharmed, his copy couldn't be defeated, and as long as the copy remained functioning, his true form needn't fear a mortal injury. But somewhere along the line the laws of physics had to be respected, and when the copy was damaged, the same spot had trouble healing on the real Nobleman.

Not even faded light leaked through the heavy forest, and the two of them were in deep shadow.

"That's decided easily enough—however, one essential question remains unsolved. Why were we brought back to life? To destroy D?"

Just as the face in the shadows took on an even darker expression, the doppelgänger stirred up a breeze as it hastened to its feet. While the grand duke knew it mimicked his every movement, it still held him spellbound.

From the depths of the forest—off to the south—a tall figure was approaching. Covered from head to toe in armor the hue of the darkness, the figure halted about thirty feet from the grand duke.

"Are you working for D?" the Nobleman inquired, even though he knew that couldn't possibly be the case. But the murderous intent that billowed at him was so far beyond the pale, he couldn't help but ask.

"He's one of your colleagues!" General Gaskell said, his words raining down from nowhere in particular.

"General?"

"He's an assassin I summoned. His name is Lord Rocambole, and—"

Whatever the great general had intended to say next was cut off by Grand Duke Mehmet's cry of surprise.

"Lord Rocambole—an atrocious fellow who was never supposed to be brought back, no matter how it might change the history of the Nobility."

"You might well call him a god of atrocity," the disembodied voice said with relish. "You and the others have disappointed me. I summoned all these vaunted figures, yet I'm terribly let down that you haven't finished off that stripling yet. Everything has to transform, from the ground up. In other words, we need a change of personnel."

"So you intend to replace me—with Rocambole? The curse of Mehmet will be on you for generations!"

"Unfortunately, you alone won't suffice. I had to throw in two more—Baron Schuma, and the Duke of Xenon's daughter. Even with this three-for-one trade, the lord seems a bit dissatisfied. He claims he requires four lives to slay D for certain."

It was unclear whether or not Gaskell's words reached him; the armored figure hadn't made a single movement. Compared to the Duke of Xenon's modern armor, his suit seemed horribly antiquated.

Now, his right hand rose. As he reached for the longsword on his hip, his movements were terribly jerky. He'd be no match for D like this. And yet, the real Mehmet leapt back a good ten feet.

"The lord is still half asleep. We haven't fulfilled the part of the contract yet where the three of you are slain. However, even in that state, he's still up to fighting you. Just try him, Grand Duke Mehmet."

"Actually, I had intended to flee," Grand Duke Mehmet said, determination filling his eyes. "But I can't step aside now, general. For my sake and the sake of the others you've summoned, Lord Rocambole must be destroyed."

"Hmm, well said. I suppose that might help shake him from his sleep. Are you fine with that, milord?"

His answer came in the form of the longsword the newcomer drew. Unlike D's curved blade, this one was straight and double edged. It was also thick. More than intricate swordsmanship, this old-fashioned sword was meant for swinging and chopping and whacking.

The gigantic doppelgänger opened its mouth. No matter what kind of skill this man might possess, Grand Duke Mehmet was convinced he couldn't be any worse than D. The way the Hunter had cut into his doppelgänger was unlike anything any foe had done before. Not only had the grand duke's true form writhed in hellish pain, but for a few seconds, he'd actually died. It didn't seem possible there was another person in the whole world with such freakish skill. Though he'd heard Lord Rocambole's name and knew of his abilities, it came as little surprise he still put more trust in what he'd physically experienced.

The space eater disgorged by his copy began to devour itself ten feet from the armored figure. The hole that opened in space roared as it sucked up everything around it.

Artlessly, the lord raised his right hand. He slashed at the hole in space. This shouldn't have had any effect at all, but the hole fell apart lengthwise. Without even glancing at the giant figure who stood there, dumbfounded, by its sudden disappearance, the lord raised his sword with his right hand and hurled it at a tree a good hundred feet away. From behind the tree came a painful death rattle, quickly replaced by silence.

While Rocambole went over to the tree with the jerky movements of a marionette, the giant behind him fell, turning into multicolored clay in a matter of seconds. But the lord never looked back at it. Grabbing the sword that had been buried to the hilt, he pulled it out again with one tug . . . and using only one hand.

Though there was the sound of something heavy falling on the opposite side, Lord Rocambole didn't seem the least bit interested as he returned his longsword to its sheath and walked back the way he'd come.

"Now there are just two more, Lord Rocambole. We shall meet soon!" General Gaskell said, his voice giving way to laughter, and then gradually fading into the distance.

Perhaps catching the stench of blood in the dark forest where not even a beam of sunlight pierced the trees, countless insects buzzed into action, but suddenly they scattered in unison. On the grass not ten feet from the fateful tree there lay a boulder, and from behind it a figure in a blaze of vermilion had appeared.

"Well, I finally manage to get that vampire bloom out of me, only to find this odd turn of events. They said something about trading three lives; all that leaves is Gillis, Lady Ann, and me. I don't know who's going to be spared, but I think it would be best if I took my leave as soon as possible."

III

The scene in the village was far worse than Juke and the others had ever imagined. For lack of a better word, it was hell. The ground, the houses, the well, the stables—everything was stained with blood. Inside and out, villagers dyed vermilion had fallen, and regardless of whether or not they still drew breath, thin geysers of blood gushed from each and every one of their pores like some sort of parlor trick.

Having no choice but to leave the dead where they lay, they went around injecting those who still lived with the medicine. Even for a village the place was still pretty big. They'd only covered a third of it by twilight, and the group had no choice but to depend on lanterns and the lights on their wagon to continue their work. Even after they'd given the people the injections, most of them were too far gone and died. On seeing the corpse of a baby that couldn't have been more than a few months old, Gordo and Sergei sobbed out loud.

Keeping away from the group while they were absorbed by their ghastly task, Lady Ann stood outside the wagon. She heard Gordo cursing and Sergei crying inside a crude house. The cute little girl couldn't understand what made them so sad.

Human beings grew old and died. She understood that. But what about a Noble like herself? Lady Ann had already lived nearly eight centuries looking exactly the same as she did now. And she would probably stay that way forever—so long as she didn't take a rough wooden stake through the heart or decay in the light of the sun. Wasn't that wonderful?

As a Noble, it was extremely difficult for Lady Ann to comprehend the grief humans felt in the face of death, and it gave her a slight feeling of superiority—or it should have. And yet, for some reason, a desolate wind blew through her heart. The way the dead girl that shared her name had looked remained now in Lady Ann's brain. Ann would never move again—she would never come back to life. How pointless. How frail. That's what it meant to be a human being. For those who died and those they left behind, death seemed something unspeakably cruel. Yet that girl—the other Ann—had worn a peaceful face in death.

Someone had once whispered something into Lady Ann's ear: *I envy human beings. Because they live as hard as they can, and die still wanting to live some more.* Come to think of it, all the Nobility Lady

Ann knew were shrouded in a kind of indolent ennui. Splendid masques and solemn plays in golden opera houses all drifted by like a lazy summer's afternoon reeking of blood and death, but for all their laughter, the Nobility were weary. They were tired. Oh so tired. But what would come next?

From the very start, Lady Ann couldn't be expected to understand the beauty of mortality, but what she did feel was vague anxiety and a pang of futility. Despite this, a ten-year-old human girl had died looking satisfied. Is that what it meant to live as hard as you could?

Gordo and Sergei's words faded into the distance, and Lady Ann felt as if she'd been cut off from the world. There weren't any stars in the sky. There wasn't even a moon.

"Lady Ann," someone called out to her.

She turned, but there was no one there.

"You can't see me in the darkness. Because the night is a world made from the shadows."

"Major General Gillis?"

"None other."

"Where are you?" the girl inquired raptly.

"At your feet."

Only darkness lay there. But if the major general said so, it was probably the case. She had no particular dislike for the man.

How did you get here? she was going to ask, but she stopped herself. For the man they called "the Dark One," night and the darkness were his own personal kingdom.

"What do you want?" she inquired out of reflex. "Don't tell me you're out to take D's life . . ."

"In the end, yes," Major General Gillis replied. "But at present, there's a more pressing matter. It concerns a woman very dear to me."

"What might that be?"

"General Gaskell has abandoned us. In exchange for the lives of three of us, he intends to dispatch a more powerful assassin. Lord Rocambole."

"Oh my," Lady Ann said, and then she lost her voice. "Of all the dastardly things to do . . ."

"You must run away."

"What?"

"I came here because of you. Your name is one of the three on his list."

"And who are the three?"

"Baron Schuma, Grand Duke Mehmet, and yourself."

Lady Ann raised a delicate eyebrow. "Which list are you on, Major General Gillis?"

"Fate will decide that."

"You alone have found favor with the great General Gaskell, it would seem."

Though young, Lady Ann had a fearsome ability to analyze and draw conclusions.

"Wait. Hear me out."

"No."

Saying this, the girl stuck her right hand into her golden hair, plucked out a number of strands, and jabbed them into the ground without any further discussion. The hairs became trenchant needles. Pulling out one that had sunk a good eight inches into the ground, she shouted as loud as she could, "Come right out here, you coward!"

"Calm yourself, Lady Ann." This time she heard him quite clearly. "I was merely concerned about your well-being—"

"You think that everyone will absolve you of your guilt, don't you? I won't be your tool!" Lady Ann exclaimed, driving one of her hair needles into the spot from which she thought his voice had come.

The following replies came in a sincere tone, each from a different spot.

"Stop it!"

"Listen to what I have to say."

"I can help you."

Though both of them lived in the world of darkness and night, the man known as the Dark One proved as elusive as the day was long.

Finally, Lady Ann shouted, "D!"

"Well, I wanted you to come along peacefully, if at all possible. I'll have to make you listen to me the 'shadow' way."

His voice faded, and a few seconds later, Lady Ann turned pitch black from the feet up, and then the lovely little Noblewoman sank right down into the ground . . . or rather, into the shadows.

Several seconds later, D rushed over to that silent region. Though he looked as hard as he could with Noble eyes that could turn darkness into midday, he could detect nothing in the gloom that spread across the ground. Moving no further, he did something strange. Drawing the longsword from his back, he thrust it into the ground in front of him. Then turning his back on the blade, he asked the darkness before him, "Can you hear me?"

After a while, a voice responded, "Yes." It was impossible to tell whether the voice rained from the heavens or rose from the earth. "I was under the belief I'd concealed my presence, but you saw through that, did you? You truly are a man to be feared. But your ability earns you my name, at least. I am Major General Gillis. They call me 'the Dark One.' We've met once before."

"What happened to the girl?"

"I've taken her. Fear not. I shall see to it that she escapes."

"Escapes?" a hoarse voice asked.

"You see, the great General Gaskell . . ." the voice began, going on to disclose the bizarre three-for-one exchange and the names of all those involved. "Well, I have my own reasons for taking the girl. It's my intent that the two of us flee together. Before I went, I thought I might take your life, but that won't be so easy after all. Thanks to that sword, I can't attack you from behind."

At D's feet, something suddenly rose like a fog, covering him all the way up to his head. Light flowed out—a gleam that shouldn't have been visible in the pitch-dark night. Two streaks of light cut through the fog, and then sank into the figure in black that leapt from it just after that. The fog vanished, and the sword was in D's hand.

Somewhere in the darkness, a voice reminiscent of a cry of pain was heard to say, "Not even my surprise attack works on you? There's more than just *this* in the Dark One's book of tricks, but I'm finished with you here and now. I'll thank you to pray for my happiness with the little lady."

The voice dwindled in the distance, disappearing before long.

D turned his gaze to the blade in his right hand. In an unusual turn of events, there was still blood on it. One swipe threw the gore to the ground at his feet. The instant it struck the earth, it spread and vanished in no time. Apparently, it was the shadow's blood.

"Lord Rocambole, of all people?" groaned a voice that wasn't D's, from near the Hunter's hip. "There's a fiend to make any Noble regret being born a member of the Nobility—a born mass murderer. Rumor has it he's the crazy bastard son of the Sacred Ancestor. And they called in someone like *that*?"

Catching its breath, D's left hand continued, "Things are gonna get a whole lot more complicated. This trip has been the worst."

The treatment continued until early the next afternoon, and the transporters were left with only eight villagers who looked like they would pull through.

"Given four or five days' rest, you should make a full recovery."

Everyone nodded at Juke's words.

"What should we do next?" one of the older villagers asked, and utter silence descended.

The village was completely cut off. No matter how the transporters might assert that the villagers had been cured of the plague, there was no way they'd be believed. Those blockaders intended to see the entire village of Hardue eradicated.

"So if they go out looking for help, they'll just get gunned down?" Juke mused, folding his arms. "In that case, there's only one thing we can do. Eh, boys?"

Gordo and Sergei both nodded.

Turning to the villagers, who'd stiffened into lumps, he said, "Relax. We'll bring you someplace safe soon enough. Are all of you ready to leave this village behind and make a new life?"

They all looked at one another. The five men and women past middle age looked anxious, but the three children had a sparkle in their eyes as one of them said, "Sure!"

Juke and D stepped outside.

"We've finally managed to save them," Juke said, sounding quite emotional.

"It's because they could see the future," D told him.

"Ain't that the truth. Children are the strength of tomorrow. I'm just trying to give them a hand."

"Get them in the wagon," D said unexpectedly. "I smell oil. Gasoline."

"What?" Juke exclaimed. As he crinkled his brow, he turned his gaze in the same direction as D's.

In the distance stood the palisade that surrounded the village, and from beyond it flew a rapid succession of arrows. Streaks of white trailed after them—flaming arrows. The instant they sank into the ground or roofs, flames spread for dozens of feet in all directions. Arrows rained down from all sides. No human being could possibly do all of this—they had to be using some kind of launchers. Those surrounding Hardue had decided to burn the village to the ground.

Since the transporters' wagon was packed with cargo, the villagers had to travel in a local wagon.

"It's no use. The first one that hits it will be the end," Sergei moaned. The fire was building, and the air was terribly hot. "Let's dump our cargo."

"We've got a job to do. We're transporters. Even if his own kid just died, a transporter delivers that cargo."

"Yeah, but—"

"I'll go with them," D said as he headed for his horse. "Don't mind us. Just go—and be quick about it."

Juke stared long and hard at the young man in black. In a voice as tight as a fist, he said, "We're counting on you, then."

"Count on us," a hoarse voice said.

By the time three flaming arrows had hit the house where the townsfolk had been treated, the wagons were racing at an incredible speed toward the village's gate. The houses and streets were already a sea of flames, and arrows continued to rain down. But not one of them reached the wagon that carried the villagers. D was covering the wagon's back, and each time his blade painted a gleaming arc, an arrow split in two, was batted away, or fell to the ground. There truly was nothing to worry about.

"The gate's shut!" Gordo shouted.

"Leave that to me," Sergei said, pounding one hand against his chest while he used his other hand to raise something.

The cleaner made a faint noise, and then the gate suddenly vanished, the waiting band of men scattering as the two wagons raced off down the road.

Ah! A little light shined through. Sunlight burst through the leaden clouds to share its blessings with them.

CHAPTER 5

I

After they'd raced three miles to the south, Juke finally halted the wagons. Everyone—even the villagers—turned to D. Though rapture glazed their eyes, this time there was more than one cause of it: his good looks—and his sword.

"We managed to break out, but the real problem is what comes next," Juke declared. "The surrounding villages have probably been notified that victims of the horrible fountain plague have escaped—meaning they can't go anywhere. If they were to go to another Frontier sector, everything would be fine, but we don't have time for that. So, what do we do?"

They all just tilted their heads to one side.

On the Frontier, people simply didn't like strangers. Even if they were to make a new village, as soon as they were discovered, the flaming arrows were sure to fly. If they couldn't settle anywhere, they'd be left no choice but to become drifters, but travelers were checked quite strictly, and people would be ready to deal with them no matter where they went.

"We have to get other villages to recognize that they've been cured," D said.

Sergei nodded and added, "Yeah. If we could do that, they could find some free land and start over again."

"There is a way."

Everyone held their breath at this, and then let out a cry of something like joy. If this young man said it, then they all believed it.

"The Frontier Medical Corps from the Capital is supposed to be making the rounds in this part of the Frontier. If they were to check these people out, they could send guarantees to all the villages ahead that there's nothing wrong with them."

"Yeah—the Medical Corps!" Gordo said, pounding his beefy chest. "That'd fix everything. If we told 'em about the situation, they'd know how to handle this."

The villagers hugged one another, and their tears began to flow.

Watching them out of the corner of his eye, Sergei whispered to Juke, "But where's the Medical Corps? We can't fall any further behind in our deliveries."

"If everything goes smoothly, we should reach the post town of Cactus by this evening," said D.

"Yeah, *if things go smoothly*."

"Then we'll leave that to heaven above," Juke declared.

Leave it to heaven above—these were usually famous last words on the Frontier.

The next thing Lady Ann knew, she was lying naked on the ground. There was rope around her hands and feet. She focused her strength on the amateurish bonds, but they wouldn't budge. It wasn't a matter of the rope being resilient, but rather a case of having lost her strength.

The location seemed to be an abandoned hut for huntsmen. The stench of the blood and gristle of beasts clung to the walls and floor. Through the broken windowpanes, a tired excuse for sunlight filtered in.

Lady Ann guessed it was shortly before dusk. She grew alarmed. The membrane the general had given her to protect her from sunlight should be losing its efficacy about now. Though she took a panicked look at her hands and feet, they weren't burnt or decaying. There weren't even any indications of such a thing starting to happen.

Just as relief came over her, a voice from the left end of the room said, "It seems you're awake."

"Major General Gillis. You certainly have some nerve," the cute little girl said, her countenance becoming that of a demoness.

"It's no use. Look at the shadows."

"What?"

Looking down at the floor, the girl was astonished. Although the light from the window illuminated her exposed abdomen and thighs, they cast no shadow.

" 'Shadow stealing' is a Dark One trick—since ancient times, it's been believed that taking someone's shadow takes her life. You can't move."

"You're right. Give it back, you coward."

"Regrettably, I can't do that. If I were to let you out of here, you'd no doubt go right back to that Hunter named D."

"Of course I would. He's my beloved, after all."

"That pains me. The truth is, I've had a thing for you since the moment I first laid eyes on you."

Lady Ann may not have been too happy to hear this outlandish confession. A few seconds later, she gasped as she looked down at her own nakedness.

"I see. So that's why I'm like this. Pervert! You're just an old lecher. Give me back my clothes!"

"Oh, I suppose I'll be able to do that a little later," the voice said in a reluctant tone. It came from the shadows at the end of the room. They had a somewhat human form to them.

"What do you mean by *later*? Oh, now I see. Seven hundred years ago, it was *you* that was spying on girls in the bath in the Capital's residential quarters and stealing their underwear, wasn't it? I'll make you pay!"

"I haven't done anything for which I need to pay, nor have I stolen any underwear. I'm just enjoying myself a little."

"Pervert! I'd sooner die than let you have your way," Lady Ann said, her eyes filled with a stern determination as she glared at the shadow at the end of the room.

The shadow looked a bit rattled by this.

"Well, what I'm doing—it's not like that. I have no intention of being imprudent, so be at ease. For my soul has been captivated by your innocent beauty."

"You've done this a lot, haven't you?"

"I'd prefer not to dwell on that matter." Coughing once, the voice then suggested, "So, would you be so good as to run away with me?"

"Have you lost your mind?"

"Listen to me. Our great general has decided to revive Lord Rocambole by sacrificing three lives, including your own. If you escape, the lord will have no choice but to fight D in a less-than-optimal condition. In other words, you would be doing something to help save the man you love."

"By joining hands with you, right? I'd rather die. Besides, even if Lord Rocambole were to destroy me, you think he could ever beat D?"

"Love is clouding your judgment in that matter."

"Shut up!" Lady Ann exclaimed, writhing.

Perhaps finding her somewhat difficult to handle, the shadow at the end of the room said, "You're a terrible little shrew. Though I must say that's part of what I like about you. If you're opposed to running off with me, I guess there's nothing more I can do. I shall have to go alone."

"Brilliant idea," Lady Ann told him, and then her eyes grew wide.

From the shadow at the end of the room, what was clearly the silhouette of a hand had slid up the wall, carefully avoiding the sunlight as it drew the blinds.

A feeble darkness ruled the hut.

"Since it's come to this, there's nothing else I can do. Rather than let a young man like him have the girl I love, I'll have my way with you right here before I reduce you to ash, which I'll put into a lovely little bottle and keep with me always. I'm sorry, but you'd best prepare yourself."

"Wait. Please, stop!"

In her panic, the girl had slipped back into polite speech. On the floor where the shadows were dense, one particularly heavy black shadow glided toward her, and the silhouette of a hand reached out to embrace the naked beauty.

"Help!" Lady Ann shrieked like a little girl, and her cowering clearly twisted the shadow's features into an expression of delight.

"Excellent!" he chortled. "Your fear is driving me wild. A mature woman in the same situation couldn't do that for me. There's nothing cute about *them* at all. Go on. I need more fear! More terror!"

The shadow's hand crept across the girl's pale thigh, moved to her waist, and then rose to her youthful breasts.

"No! Stop! Don't! Father!" Lady Ann sobbed on the cold wooden floor.

The sexual deviant couldn't have asked for a more arousing sight. His other hand slid around to her derrière.

"Stop it!" she shouted, but her mouth was covered by that of the black shadow.

Lady Ann looked like some small, unfortunate animal caught in the coils of a perfectly flat serpent.

A second later, the Dark One—Major General Gillis—cried, "Oof!" as he leapt away. It wasn't so much a leap back as it was a matter of the shadows on the floor retreating, but something else moved: a single crimson bloom. Lady Ann's skill with supernatural flowers still worked. It pierced the two-dimensional shadow in a three-dimensional manner.

"You—you little minx!" the shadow bellowed. His anger was prompted by an undisguisable agony. "You shall pay for that. I'll tear you to pieces before I have my way with you!"

"We'll see about that, you pervy bastard," Lady Ann jeered.

Though the unclad girl looked to be only ten, she was a peerless warrior who'd risked her life for centuries in battle.

"Lucky for me you didn't know what my power was. Did you think I was just a naked little brat? I have one more kill to my credit than my father did! Now be a good little boy and let my flower feed on you."

Gillis groaned in pain.

The bloody bloom grew out of the floor, its petals turning blacker and blacker. It was drinking, absorbing the shadow's blood.

And then the light within the hut faded rapidly. Something huge had passed by the window outside. Major General Gillis's shadow melted into these new shadows—and by the time sunlight had returned to the window, a reddish black flower lay on the floor.

Lady Ann bit her lip. She had a foreboding of Gillis's next attack. However, she heard no triumphant laugh or angry shouts. It appeared that wherever he lay in the hut's shadows, the Dark One now focused his attention on someone other than Lady Ann.

The wooden door opened. And the form so massive it made the interior of the hut seem cramped was that of none other than the great General Gaskell.

General! Major General Gillis was about to cry out, but apparently Gaskell already knew where he was, because he looked to the north wall of the room and said, "While you are in my domain, there's nowhere to run from me, Major General Gillis. We've taken Grand Duke Mehmet's life, but I don't know where Schuma is. Even factoring in the Duke of Xenon's child, we're still short one."

"My good general—you wouldn't," the major general said, his voice choked with fright. He understood very well what Gaskell was driving at. "It was *I* who came up with this whole idea. Great general though you are, if you were to do such a thing to me, your name would live in infamy for future generations."

"It already does," Gaskell said with a wry smile. In that respect, there was something strangely human about him. "But there is something to what you say. Let's do this, then. Go find Baron Schuma. Do so, and it will keep you off the list."

"With pleasure," the shadow said.

Then, as if something had suddenly occurred to him, he asked, "What will you do with this girl?"

II

You could say the matter the transporters had left to heaven above had been left in very good hands.

In the evening light, the group arrived at the post town of Cactus to learn that the Frontier Medical Corps had arrived about three hours earlier and had set up a temporary hospital on the outskirts of town. Bringing the eight villagers there, the transporters explained the situation, and while the men in the corps were astonished at first, the villagers were now in the hands of doctors who traveled the Frontier. Quickly performing examinations, the doctors gave within thirty minutes their expert opinion that all of the villagers had been completely cured of fountain plague. Putting the survivors up in their hospital, the doctors also said they'd send word of their findings to the surrounding villages.

Juke and the others happily shook each other's hands, while the eight villagers wept for joy.

Returning to their inn in high spirits, they found someone in a second-story window calling down to them, "Hi, folks!"

Looking up, all of them—including D—had surprise in their eyes.

Leaning out of a roofed passageway, wearing a pair of pink pajamas and waving to them, was Baron Schuma.

Five minutes later, they all met in the lobby. Aside from D, the group was bristling with murderous intent, but the baron told them to settle down and asserted that he no longer had any intention of fighting them. The reason, according to the baron, was "because the great general is out to take our lives."

When D asked if he was talking about Rocambole, the baron couldn't conceal his surprise.

"My, but you are good. Grand Duke Mehmet was killed before my very eyes. Lady Ann and I will be next. Like the saying goes—where there's life, there's hope."

"What are you doing here?"

At D's query the Nobleman shrugged his shoulders. "No matter how I might try to run, I can't go beyond a certain range. I must be caught in the general's drifting domain. If that's the case, there's no point losing my head about it. Besides, the hot spring at this inn has quite a reputation."

"This is one odd bird," Gordo remarked.

"As long as I remain in the general's domain, Rocambole will come for me sooner or later. I don't intend to die easily. D—will you help me?"

"This is all too convenient," said a cool voice that carried not the slightest concern for the life of a foe.

"I thought you'd feel that way," the baron said, smacking the back of his neck a few times and getting to his feet. "After bringing us back to life, he has no problem with disposing of us once we no longer suit his needs. Who in the world decided that was to be our fate?"

The baron left with a desolate hue coloring his eyes.

D went outside. He intended to take in the night air. Shadow and light—this young man belonged to both, but given his Noble blood, it came as no surprise that the darkness of night brought the most out of his good looks.

"D!"

The trio was coming up behind the Hunter on the street. Off in the distance, the strains of a guitar could be heard. It was playing a song called "Whenever and Wherever."

"We have a job—well, really, it's more of a request," Juke said, looking back at the other two. "It concerns the squirt—Lady Ann. Could you do something to save her?"

Saying nothing, D stared at the faces of the men.

"You see—the three of us talked it over. I don't know all the ins and outs, but at this rate, she'll wind up getting killed. If possible, we'd like you to rescue her."

"This is the same girl who tried to kill you," D remarked, his eyes on Gordo.

The bearded man nodded his head. Looking D straight in the eye, he said, "I know that. She's a real piece of work, but she's traveled with us the past few days. And knowing she'll be killed, we just can't leave her to her fate."

"If you don't wanna do it, we won't force you to. We just thought maybe there was a chance you would. Sorry. Forget we mentioned it."

Clapping D on the shoulder, Juke headed back to the inn with the other transporters.

"Ain't they a strange bunch," the Hunter's left hand remarked in a suspicious tone. "After spending a day or two with the same little girl who tried to kill them, they go and ask you to save her—sure are a bunch of softies . . . Huh?"

On witnessing something strange, the hoarse voice stopped speaking.

D was silently gazing at the backs of the three weary men. A smile had begun to form on his lips. If Juke, Gordo, or Sergei had looked over his shoulder at that point, he would've told people for the rest of his life about how he'd put it there. It was just such a smile.

A clamor went up on the street. As this was a post town, most of the buildings on either side of the road were hotels, inns, or places where travelers might be entertained. Even after the sun had gone down, there was still a lot of foot traffic. But in unison the pedestrians had turned their eyes to the opposite end of the street from where D was, and then rushed into the nearest buildings to take shelter. As if a black tide were rolling over them, one shop after another extinguished its lights.

D could already feel with every inch of his body the murderous intent billowing toward him. The lust for killing that had driven even ordinary humans to evacuate radiated from the statuesque armored figure coming from the far end of the street.

"It's Lord Rocambole," his left hand said. "Probably here to do away with Baron Schuma. Better not get mixed up in this. If you do, he'll just take off."

But as if to mock what the hoarse voice had said, Lord Rocambole halted about forty or fifty feet from the Hunter.

"Interesting," said a voice that was somehow unsteady. "I've already slain the one known as Mehmet. Two more and I shall live again. Yet here's a man who by himself would suffice. I am Lord Rocambole. What name do you go by?"

"D."

"Oh?" the armored figure exclaimed in surprise. "D—I've been summoned to take care of a man by that name."

D didn't move. The exchange between the pair consisted of words alone.

An evening scene in a peaceful post town—who knew it could be transformed into a battlefield heavy with the shadow of death? No one save warriors might survive here.

"Hey!" someone called out behind D.

In front of the entrance to an inn stood a man wearing vermilion clothes and a top hat and carrying a walking stick, a devilish grin on his face.

"And here's another one—D, we shall meet again," said the armored figure. Then, with a gait that suggested he'd forgotten all about D, he walked toward his second target—Baron Schuma.

"This should be something to see," the hoarse voice said with relish, as if they were going to watch a play.

D remained still. Saying nothing, he watched the two men. He'd already seen the baron do his thing at Jalha Station—this man could make his opponents stop and cause blood to gush from their throats without any physical contact at all. No matter how the Hunter's left hand might've feared this Lord Rocambole, one had to wonder if the armored figure could stand up to such a bizarre ability.

The baron's walking stick rose with a smooth movement.

Rocambole halted.

"The baron's setting the pace," said the hoarse voice.

Breathless observers were congregating in the entrances to darkened shops and hotels. They swallowed hard as they stared at the pair, yet the victor was to be decided with stunning simplicity.

The baron's stick zipped to the right.

The lord's throat popped open. Perhaps it wasn't even a wound.

The lord took a step forward. The spectators imagined the baron leaping away. In fact, he did make a leap.

Lord Rocambole drew his sword from his hip. Aiming it at the baron, who was still high in the air, he swung it. Then he did so twice more.

The baron landed.

"I've taken your measure," Schuma said with a wry grin. "And you can't beat D. He's all yours, Hunter!"

Three crimson lines shot through his body, and the baron fell to the ground in six separate pieces. An unbelievable amount of fresh blood spilled out onto the street, soaking the ground like a passing shower.

"Hmm," a voice croaked from the vicinity of D's hip, sounding suitably impressed. The baron's death had been that stunning.

He, too, had been connected to D—tied by the invisible strings of some unknown puppet master. Yet the one who'd cut those strings didn't appear to have any feelings regarding the gorgeous Hunter. The death match that had lasted mere seconds was over, and the armored figure still stood on the road, not even letting out a sigh as he brought the hand that held his sword to his throat. With one touch the wound vanished.

"That makes two . . . D, we'll meet again after I've finished with the third."

D responded, "About that—I can't let you kill her."

When he took a step forward, the air on the street congealed with a new tension—far more intense than what had come before.

Ten feet separated D and Lord Rocambole. This alone measured the length of one of their lives. Like Baron Schuma, this Nobleman had the ability to slay a foe without his blade ever touching—so victory would have to be seized before he ever moved his sword.

When D's blade danced out to reflect the darkness, Lord Rocambole assumed a posture to parry it. He raised his left arm to meet the blow. There was a dull thud that wasn't just the sound of armor being pierced. Though people saw the arm fall in the street, they didn't witness D's blade reversing direction to sink into the lord's chest.

Sparks scattered with a beautiful sound.

As the armored figure made a great leap back, an almost plaintive cry went through the crowd, although not even they knew why that was.

Even after his left arm had been severed, Lord Rocambole had met D's second blow with one of his own. The blade limned an arc. D had been in no position to dodge the mysterious attack. From the left side of his neck to his right lung a streak that was black even to night sight shot through him, with fresh blood spraying out as if to make a desperate escape. He fell to one knee on the street.

It was still Rocambole's turn to be on the offensive. However, the armored figure who'd parried D's blow lowered his sword and staggered a bit. Losing that arm had probably damaged him more than he knew.

Stained reddish black from the chest down, D got up again.

Lord Rocambole's sword also rose.

No sooner had the people drawn a deep breath in expectation of the next life-or-death spectacle than they heard a rumbling and the rattling of wheels approaching. A black carriage drawn by enormous horses appeared from the same end of the road from which Lord Rocambole had come.

D and Lord Rocambole leapt back, and both were left reeling again from their grievous injuries.

The carriage stopped between them. It was so huge it'd mercilessly ripped down signs and shaved the eaves off buildings on either side

of the road. The person who stepped from its door was clearly none other than the great General Gaskell.

Taking a long, hard look at the two men, one to either side of him, the general said with very real admiration, "I had a bad feeling about this and came as fast as I could, but this really is most incredible. However, it shall have to be settled next time. D—I have the girl. Will you come and see if you can rescue her before Lord Rocambole has recovered from his wounds?"

Jabbing a finger at the darkened western sky, he continued, "You remember where my castle is, I take it? We'll be waiting in the front courtyard. Needless to say, I won't mind if you don't come, either. Get in, Lord Rocambole."

The pair climbed in and shut the door—and at that instant, D sprang. After his blade sank into the roof of the carriage and slashed at an angle through half of the door that had nearly closed, the Hunter once again dropped to one knee.

"My castle. I'll be waiting for you!" the great general said, his shouts giving way to mocking laughter an instant before the carriage dissolved into the darkness.

When D started walking to where his steed was tethered, Sergei ran over to him. His face pale, the transporter said, "We've got a problem. While we were watching you guys fighting, Rosaria disappeared."

III

Carrying a woman in a negligee, the horse galloped single-mindedly down the highway in the one direction it shouldn't have been going. Travelers on Frontier roads were generally few and far between as it approached midnight, but if there had been any around, they probably wouldn't have noticed her wardrobe half as much as the fact that her arms were wrapped around the horse's neck instead of holding the reins and that she was slumped forward against the beast. She might've been out riding and had an accident, only to have her startled steed race along madly—but that couldn't be it, as her horse's gait was too controlled, and no animal would keep going this long with its rider unconscious.

Even if someone had noticed that a black shadow clung tight to the woman's back, and that long, thin shapes that seemed like hands seemed to reach for the reins, he never could've imagined that the shadow possessed a will of its own and was controlling the rampaging animal. It was Major General Gillis who'd kidnapped Rosaria from the inn.

In no time he came to Castle Gaskell, towering in the darkness. From the front courtyard to the great hall, Rosaria used her own two feet, but only because Major General Gillis still clung to her and worked them for her.

"So glad you made it back," Gaskell said, his voice seeming to issue from the heavens and the earth, and with that Major General Gillis pulled free of Rosaria. Finally, Rosaria fell to the floor.

"As promised, I've returned with a replacement. Don't tell me Lady Ann has already been—"

"She's over there."

They heard a door opening off to the right. Behind it stood Lady Ann, now in a white dress. The look she gave Major General Gillis—or rather, the shadow that lay on the floor—burned with hatred and repulsion.

"The love of your life has returned, Lady Ann," the great general teased.

"Kindly stop that. You've taken this joke too far," the girl said in a tone devoid of even the tiniest bit of warmth.

"What a callous thing to say. The peerless assassin known as the Dark One has stooped to kidnapping, all for your sake."

"It's only natural, as I love another. Even if he might never love me in return," the girl said, each and every word viciously barbed.

"As we agreed back in the hunting shack, I've brought you back a replacement for Lady Ann. Now you can sacrifice her instead to awaken Lord Rocambole and—"

"Ah, if only I could."

"What?" the shadow on the floor exclaimed, shaking violently.

"The woman you brought back won't serve as a replacement. You see, she isn't one of the assassins I selected."

"Wait. Why didn't you tell me that before?"

"Because, for some reason, I have need of that woman. Sooner or later, I had to get her back here. And you were able to help me with that. However, I can't use her in Lady Ann's place."

"You've tricked me, Gaskell!" Major General Gillis bellowed in anger. "We must flee, Lady Ann—you mustn't remain here!"

The shadow glided over to the girl's feet. He started to rise up over her toes—and then fell back to the floor.

Lady Ann had suddenly vanished.

"A holograph, Major General Gillis," Gaskell jeered. "And if you didn't notice as much, then your sick infatuation must've affected your eyesight. Ha! Who knew there were deviants even among the shadows? However, now that Schuma's and Mehmet's lives have been taken, we need only one more to make Lord Rocambole one of us. So, would you care to go in her stead?"

The general's laughter continued for a short while, but then it ended abruptly. Major General Gillis had started to laugh as well.

He said, "No, I'm not especially proud of the way I acted. When you come right down to it, there's no life I value more than my own. I'll be more than happy to let you have Lady Ann."

"That's what's known as discretion," Gaskell's voice remarked. "Since we've taken the two women, D is sure to come here. I couldn't be sure about Lady Ann alone, but he'll do it as long as he's still working as a guard for the men with that cargo wagon. Lord Rocambole and I should be more than a match for him, but how about you, Gillis—will you aid us?"

"With pleasure."

"In that case—wait in your room. I have some arrangements to make to prepare for our guest."

"What of Lady Ann?"

"Still not over her yet? That's understandable. In recognition of your love for the girl, we shall hold off on offering her life to the lord until D comes."

"That's most generous of you," the shadow said, donning a despicable expression.

Then, in an even more despicable tone, he said, "Before then, if at all possible, I'd like to—at least once, that is."

"Very well," said the voice from the ceiling. This time, it had a ring of lechery and scorn to it. "Before we take her life, you may *express your feelings* for her. Lady Ann is at the summit of the Red Tower."

As soon as he heard Rosaria had been abducted, D readied to set out. Ordinarily that would consist of just checking the hooves of his cyborg horse, which hardly seemed like preparing for battle, but this time was different. When the transporter trio called on D's room, he was scrutinizing the blade of the sword he'd kept drawn.

Entering when he told them they could, Juke and the others swallowed hard at the daunting solemnity of his expression. However, D quickly sheathed his sword.

"I'm off," was all he said. He didn't sound like it had required the least bit of resolve.

"You mean to tell me you'll go?" Juke said, giving him a doleful look.

"We've got a contract," D replied.

"Sorry. We end up saddling you with everything."

"Don't worry about it. Humans are powerless against someone of that nature. This is my job."

The whole group went outside. At some point the clouds had broken, and above them was a sky filled with stars.

D mounted his steed in front of the inn. The young man had nothing to say in parting. He made an easy wave of his right hand. And with that, he wheeled his horse around.

"Oh, that's one heck of a starry sky," the hoarse voice said.

Galloping off with the sound of hoofbeats ringing in the air, the black horse and rider were soon swallowed by the darkness.

With nothing to say, the three men silently stood beneath the star-filled heavens.

Grunting, the great General Gaskell opened a heavy door. He was in the basement of the Storage Tower, which stood at the southern end of the castle. Despite its name, all the really dangerous items and valuable treasures were kept in another location. The enormous, ten-foot-thick door and the walls that surrounded it were made of the same ultra-high-density steel. Rumor had it that the only things that could destroy this vault were an antiproton bomb or the curse of the Sacred Ancestor.

While listening to the groan of the door shutting behind him, Gaskell saw the sofa that had been placed in the center of this vast chamber and the figure that lay on it. The sight startled him.

Antiproton cannons, dimensional-shift generators, carcinogenic creatures, simulacra for curses—enough weapons to kill everything on the planet a hundred times over had been moved to a different location out of fear of a psychotic incident. The fanaticism of a single Noble might destroy the world. Of course, that one Noble alone was enough to destroy the world already.

"Lord Rocambole," Gaskell called out from thirty feet away. Honestly, he didn't want to get too close to this particular Nobleman.

The figure on the sofa slowly turned in his direction. His armor had been removed and discarded on the floor. He wore a white shirt and scarf, as well as white riding breeches. His young, well-formed face was conspicuous for its awful pallor. The eyes that reflected Gaskell filled with a reason they had lacked before.

"General Gaskell?" he replied in a lethargic tone.

"Correct. You've received two of the three lives. Only one to go—there are two prospects for that. I leave it to you to decide which it shall be."

Though the Gaskell reflected in his blue eyes grinned despicably, the young man—Lord Rocambole—merely changed the direction he faced sleepily.

Presently, he said in a low voice, "The next thing I knew, I'd been given life again—not that I particularly wanted it, but now that I have it, I'm loath to discard it. My good general, where are these girls?"

"Would you like to meet them?"

"The last two were men—but I should like to see what sort of girl is going to revive me. I really must thank her."

"And then kill her when you're done," the great general said with a casual irony. "Let us go, then. I shall introduce you to them."

The general headed for the door.

"Before we do—"

These words made Gaskell halt. But he didn't seem unnerved.

"—I should like to test myself against you."

Gaskell turned around.

Lord Rocambole stood by the sofa. His right hand was lowered, but in it gleamed a longsword.

As Gaskell gazed at the Nobleman, his eyes flooded with an intense gleam. He, too, was an intrepid and resolute warrior.

"Good enough. But since you've challenged me, this will be more than simple sparring!" he spat somewhat unreasonably, his psyche already focused on Lord Rocambole's destruction.

Neither made the first move; rather, they drew in unison. The glowing blue longsword and the huge black blade easily twice its size squared off some fifteen to twenty feet from each other. What kind of arc would the ends of those blades trace? Enormous and chilly, the room had seemed to brim with gloom from the very beginning—but now it was strung with tension.

Just which of them started to close the gap first was impossible to say. In the center of the floor between them there was a mellifluous ring and a shower of sparks. Narrowly parrying Gaskell's jab, the longsword slid closer without making a sound. Blocking it with the armored back of his left gauntlet, the great general made a series of thrusts.

Up until the third, they traded blow for blow—but perhaps not feeling up to this, Lord Rocambole leapt back a good fifteen feet. He landed. And Gaskell was right in front of him. They'd leapt the very same distance simultaneously.

"That was Baron Schuma's special skill—shame on you for appropriating it."

As the general said this, a white light appeared in this chamber that was supposedly inviolate. The lightning Gaskell launched had pierced Lord Rocambole.

A youthful face wracked by pain. A sneering grin from another half hidden by an iron mask. And then there was a new expression— Rocambole broke into a smile.

Gaskell was astounded. From head to foot, the general felt the same blistering heat and numbing shock Rocambole had felt. In his astonishment, he stopped discharging lightning.

With white smoke rising from every inch of him, Lord Rocambole said softly, "So, this is *your* secret skill, General?"

Destroyed from Within

CHAPTER 6

I

In the gloom, Lady Ann was thinking about D. Barring a miracle, she wouldn't be able to escape from her present predicament. Most likely she felt nothing but satisfaction at having saved D when he was immobilized—that was good. There was no disputing the fact she'd helped a man who would've died. Perhaps that young man didn't care a whit about Lady Ann. Nevertheless, she'd done all that she could.

"Lady Ann," someone called out to her, but the girl made no attempt to turn in the voice's direction. The young man in black still held a feverish dominion over her heart.

"Lady Ann."

The second time, she finally opened her eyes, due more to the voice that was calling her than the fact that she was being called.

In front of the locked door, the shadow that fell on the floor of the murky room was that of Major General Gillis.

"I've disabled the surveillance system and alarms. Now it's time to flee."

"You're a strange one, aren't you, to—" Lady Ann said, breaking off. She didn't know the outcome of the little experiment General Gaskell had done on Major General Gillis.

Out of love for his own life, the major general had sold out Lady Ann. However, it seemed that his disappointing compliance had all been an act. He'd decided to adopt an attitude that sickened even himself in order to deceive Gaskell so he could then rescue the young girl. Though his love was rather warped when compared to ordinary circumstances, there was certainly something to be said for the way he was willing to gamble his own life to save Lady Ann.

Perhaps Lady Ann knew as much, because though she still seemed half stunned and hateful, she also couldn't help but sound impressed as she murmured, "How did you get in here?"

"A shadow has no thickness. If I were so inclined, I could even slip into the Sacred Ancestor's bedroom. Now, there are some preparations to see to before we take flight."

"What do you mean by 'preparations'?"

"Can you move?"

"Yes," Lady Ann replied, standing up.

"Then take your clothes off."

"Excuse me?"

"I wish to claim part of my reward right here. Take your clothes off," the shadow said, his voice rising. The whole situation had clearly aroused him. The very thought of getting a reluctant girl to strip down while every second counted in making their escape! Lady Ann was entirely justified in cursing him.

"You dirty old man!" she spat. "What do you mean by 'part of your reward'?"

"That reward would be—you," the major general's shadow said. "But for now, I'll settle for a look."

"You intend to take more than that, do you?"

"We can discuss that—later."

"There's no need to discuss anything! If those are your conditions, I'm staying right here."

"You fool! Naught but death awaits you if you remain. Rocambole lacks my appreciation of beauty and won't be as gentle as I am."

"You're not gentle; you're a deviant! A sick bastard like you—"
The girl broke off there, and then continued, "I'd rather stay here

and have Lord Rocambole kill me than take orders from a deluded sex fiend."

"Rocambole is out to get D."

The shadow's words froze Lady Ann solid.

"That's the reason he's been revived. And if you stick around and help awaken him fully, you'll be sending the strongest possible foe at D. Is that what you want?"

Lady Ann looked as if she'd fallen into hell. To her, Major General Gillis's words must've sounded like a thin thread dangled down from heaven above.

"So far, he's only absorbed the lives of two warriors. If you and I run off, he'll be forced to fight D while still half asleep, in which case D will win. Rocambole wouldn't have a chance. But if he awakens completely—D will be no match for him."

"You're wrong!" Lady Ann shouted, her body trembling. "He *will* win. The man I love will never be defeated, no matter how dire the situation might be. And if he is defeated—then I will perish along with him."

For a while, the shadow maintained his silence. It was clear that shock had stopped his heart and choked his vocal cords.

"Okay, I see," Gillis said with resignation. "If you feel that strongly about him, there's nothing more I can do. Do as you like. I'll be leaving now, too. But I must ask you this one last time. Lady Ann, have you no intention at all of escaping with me?"

"Not a hair."

"I see. I have no desire to watch you die. I'll be leaving now."

"Fine," the girl replied in a remorseless manner.

Saying nothing more, the shadow that represented Major General Gillis went to the crack under the door, and in no time at all he'd disappeared through it.

Letting out another sigh, Lady Ann lay down on the floor. Her thoughts were with D again. If she closed her eyes, a face of unearthly beauty was there gazing at her softly. The look it gave her was gentler than that of the real one.

Her body tensed for a moment. A black shadow had suddenly come up behind her and attached itself to her back. It was the shadow of Major General Gillis, who'd slipped back in through the same gap under the door that he'd used to leave. Before she could do anything, Lady Ann found herself paralyzed. She couldn't say a word. Not only that, but when the shadow got up, she stood up, too. No, it's probably better in this case to say that when *Lady Ann* got up, the shadow did, too.

At any rate, as Lady Ann approached the door with robotic steps, in her ear she heard Major General Gillis say in a low voice, "Oh, I couldn't really leave the object of my affection to die here. I've undone the lock. So go. Or rather, the two of us shall head out into a new world clinging to one another."

There was no sign of anyone in the corridor. As they were about to head for the staircase, they heard the sound of numerous footsteps coming up from below. And what should appear but featureless silver beings dressed as servants. Their smooth faces lacked eyes, noses, and mouths. They were androids.

When Nobles selected servants, many of those with more volatile tempers chose androids for the machines' complete obedience. Human beings and others of their own kind tended to rub them the wrong way.

"Come to take my lady love?" Major General Gillis muttered, but by that time the androids had spotted Lady Ann and were moving toward her with powerful strides.

"You lousy piles of scrap!" the shadow laughed, and balling his hand into a fist, he drove it into Lady Ann's stomach.

Spotting the shadow as he slipped from the girl's limp, collapsing body to the floor, the androids fired purple particle beams at him from their foreheads. Leaving only those holes they'd burned in the floor, the shadow sped toward the androids' feet. Lacking physical form, could a shadow even be destroyed?

Clinging to the androids' feet, the shadow made his way up their torsos and then slipped off their backs. When he'd returned to the floor, the androids, which had been run through with a blade lacking density, began to convulse violently, black smoke billowing from their collars and wrists. Frozen in place, the first one let its head drop lifelessly, and then a second android began to twitch as well. It took less than ten seconds for five of the automatons to be reduced to scrap.

Creeping across the ground, the shadow, who'd dropped Lady Ann with ungodly speed, returned to her back. Lady Ann's eyes opened and the girl got up, but still she didn't speak. And then she saw the figure in deep purple who stood just behind the androids' remains.

"General Gaskell!"

"But that voice . . . Ah, I see. Major General Gillis has taken possession of you, has he?" the great general said, a very human surprise filling his one visible eye. "So, my authority means nothing now? If I let no more than a Nobleman with a penchant for assassination defy me, the ignominy will haunt me for all time. I must take my revenge—are you prepared to face that, Major General Gillis?"

"I am."

Lady Ann's eyes went wide—the voice had come from her own mouth.

"But when you kill me, General, let me serve as the third sacrifice to fully restore Rocambole. And in return, I should like to ask that the legacy of Roland, the Duke of Xenon—my own beloved Lady Ann—be spared."

"Oh? You would give your own life so that this girl might be allowed to leave?"

Extending one hand, Gaskell shoved the android standing in front of him to one side. Hitting the wall, it fell to the floor not with the rattle of metal but rather with the thud of a lump of clay. Its face had been knocked out of shape.

"Precisely," Major General Gillis said, and then he—or rather, Lady Ann—took a step back. There was nowhere to retreat to—it was a dead end. The only way out was a single window, and outside was a sheer drop of three hundred feet down the wall.

"You know, I can't believe it," Gaskell said, continuing to advance. To either side of him an android smashed into the wall.

"What? That at the age of 453 I've found my one true love?"

Taking several steps back, Lady Ann finally found herself beside the window. Her eyes were tinged with terror. Although a drop from any height wouldn't normally give an immortal Noble the slightest pause, she seemed to have an irrationally powerful fear.

"That's a touching sentiment," Gaskell said, crushing the last pair of androids to either side of him. "However, when you fall now to my hand, it won't be for Lord Rocambole. It will be purely because you've betrayed me. Therefore, the girl will have to be used as the last sacrifice to raise Lord Rocambole."

"That's fiendish!"

"That's the law of the Frontier."

"Of course. But I don't much care for it. You always were just a bumpkin Noble."

Gaskell's hand went for the hilt of his black sword. Behind his prey, there was nowhere to run. But his certainty of this made his movements too slow.

"What's this?" he gasped, his blade streaking from its scabbard to mow through the space in front of the window, but Lady Ann and the Dark One that clung to her back had thrown themselves out the window some three hundred feet from the ground.

II

Lady Ann screamed. But her death cry only resounded in her head. She fainted.

However, she didn't fall. Still attached to Lady Ann, Major General Gillis's limbs reached out to grab the tower's outer wall, and they began to descend like a lizard or some similar reptile.

Leaning out of the same window, General Gaskell shouted a single invective and hurled a short sword that scored twenty feet of the rock wall, but Lady Ann and the Dark One easily dodged it and reached the ground in no time.

Standing and turning to look back at the tower, Lady Ann laughed with Major General Gillis's voice. But that laughter was cut short when he saw that the great General Gaskell had leapt from the same window he and his love had used.

"Damnation!" the shadow shouted before sliding from Lady Ann's back to her front side. She then leaned forward.

Having controlled Lady Ann's body up until now, the Dark One now carried her on his back as he began to run at an impressive clip. He moved with such unholy swiftness, it was as if the darkness creeping across the earth were his own body. Actually, if the darkness shared the same density that he did, then this probably would've been true. However, Castle Gaskell had lamplight spilling from the windows and illumination in the gardens, and countless other artificial light sources, and until he could reach somewhere the light didn't hit directly, the dimness would be a weaker hue. The range of darkness under Major General Gillis's control was limited to his own size.

There was a courtyard in front of the tower. By the time Gillis reached the center of it, General Gaskell was just picking himself up from his own fall.

We're going to make it, Major General Gillis thought to himself with absolute conviction.

From the ground ahead, waves surged toward him. Rather uncharacteristically, Gillis made no attempt at a sudden stop, and the instant the waves touched him he halted, feeling as if every inch of his body had been ripped open.

I almost forgot about the other one, he thought.

Some sixty feet away stood the armored figure. The waves of murderous intent that emanated from the lord's body continued to tear at Major General Gillis.

Impatience goaded Gillis on, for he could sense the presence of General Gaskell in the distance to his rear. The great general gave off an aura every bit as unearthly as he closed on his prey.

"General," Lord Rocambole said. Unlike Gillis, he didn't refer to Gaskell as *milord*. "Is either one okay? There are two of them."

"It matters not to me," the great General Gaskell replied, but he seemed a bit ill tempered. Apparently he would've preferred to be called *milord*. "However, if at all possible, make it the woman. I will dispose of Major General Gillis. Originally you wanted four lives, but you shall have to settle for three when you do battle with D."

"Ah, the truth comes out," Gillis laughed cheerfully—apparently he'd made up his mind. "Aren't you forgetting something, milord? Has it slipped your mind that, along with Dr. Gretchen, I was also called 'a Noble killer'?"

In the darkness, a turbulent hue skimmed across Gaskell's vicious scowl. But the Dark One was faster in zipping across the earth. With the black shadow wrapped around it, Gaskell's body arched so far backward he smashed the back of his head against the ground. Though this didn't seem likely to have any effect on this giant of a man who'd just gotten up from a three-hundred-foot fall, the general was knocked out cold. And then the shadow stuck to his back slipped through Gaskell's chest.

"Aaaah!" the great general cried, loosing a scream of agony more horrible than any cry he'd made in any deadly battle before, no matter how ghastly. Several seconds later, black blood spilled from his collar and chest, from his cuffs and between his buttons. Still unconscious, he bent backward and writhed in pain. His limbs twisted in impossible directions as he twitched to the dance of death.

Pulling away from Gaskell's body, the shadow turned toward Lord Rocambole, who remained standing stock still.

Whistling through the wind, a gleam of black flew through the air to skewer Gillis's shadow as he raced across the ground. The shadow flowed like water, leaving only the black sword behind. He moved from the soles of the stationary lord to his legs. From his legs, the shadow climbed to his trunk—and now he planned to finish Rocambole with a single blow!

However, just as he was about to do so, the most terrifying thing occurred. With the deadly shadow wrapped around it, Rocambole's body collapsed to the ground—but not because Gillis's power had rendered Rocambole unconscious.

"B-but you're . . ." Major General Gillis stammered, his bewilderment quite natural. After all, how could his opponent have the same special power that he did?

As the two shadows tangled in their deadly clash, Lady Ann's vacant gaze alone watched them. Suddenly, the pair pulled apart. One of the shadows let out an ear-shattering groan of pain. And the other shadow slid smoothly over to Lady Ann, slipping into the space between her body and the ground and carrying the girl with daunting speed toward the door to the nearest garden.

However—in the feeble darkness of the garden, a long, thin streak made a black sweep along the same path as Lady Ann.

"The bleeding's quite bad," Lady Ann muttered. But as the girl was still unconscious, the words came in Major General Gillis's voice. "He's not used to dealing with shadows. I managed to get the drop on him, but he'll probably be after us soon—and it doesn't look like I can last much longer. In which case . . ."

Lady Ann stopped moving. She was practically at the center of the vast rear courtyard—on a marble pathway.

A shadowy figure emerged from beneath the girl's hunched-over form. The profile looked to be that of a man, and gazing intently at Lady Ann, he said, "I've managed to save you somehow, but this is as far as I can take you. Though I die here, I have no regrets, milady. I'm happy to have met a girl like you . . . but I can't just leave you to be sacrificed to Rocambole. Before it comes to that, I'd rather you died by my hand."

The shadow must've been drawing on the last of his strength, because as he moved toward Lady Ann, he seemed to be in a horrible kind of slow motion. His hand stretched for the girl's form. Anyone the Dark One passed through—even the great general himself—would feel her body burn with hellish torment. Lady Ann's destruction was assured.

His outstretched hand crept up Lady Ann's chest—and then it twitched violently. The torso of the shadow that lay on the ground had the shadow of a longsword running through its heart and out its back. The arm that gripped the weapon was visible from the elbow up, and it belonged to Lord Rocambole, who was kneeling on the ground. When he drew it back, both his hand and the longsword returned to their original form.

"You . . . son of a bitch . . ."

Though Major General Gillis's groan was weak, it still left the lord stunned. His deadly attack had clearly gone right through the major general's heart, and it should've killed him instantaneously. This was true tenacity. A crazed devotion to Lady Ann kept the dead man from expiring.

"I won't let you . . . have her . . . This girl . . . is mine."

Easily fending off the two arms that reached for him, Rocambole put the tip of his blade against the ground. It turned into a shadow and made another thrust at Gillis's shadow.

Major General Gillis bent backward and shook with one final spasm. That was the end of him.

Getting up, Lord Rocambole went over to Lady Ann and put the end of his longsword against her bosom. The steely tip pressed into the flesh of her chest. Pulling it away, Lord Rocambole said, "She's a lovely girl. And as I recall, there's one more. It's not too late to compare the two and see which is more beautiful."

And then he turned his eyes to the outline of the castle that towered in the distance.

†

Major General Gillis's attack far surpassed anything the great General Gaskell had experienced or could even comprehend. One by one the cells of his body burned and melted—he suffocated, he felt like vomiting, he groaned and writhed in pain. His brain had died, and his heart and lungs had completely ceased functioning. It took ten minutes for him to come back to life.

"Need . . . liquid," Gaskell muttered, raising his left forearm and sinking his teeth into it. Black blood spilled out. He drank it all up like a man stranded in the desert, swallowing at least a quart.

When he finally paused to catch his breath and wipe his lips, someone far behind him asked, "Satisfied now?"

Making an involuntary leap forward, he twisted around and landed some fifteen feet away out of surprise and fear that someone could come up behind him without his noticing, regardless of how he might've hungered. He had to wonder just how the owner of the voice had gotten there.

"D?"

Astride a cyborg horse sat a vision of beauty, and behind him one of the supposedly impassable gates was open wide.

"How did you get through the gates to my castle? Who the hell are you?"

"Where are Lady Ann and Rosaria?" All D did was ask the obvious question.

"One is in the basement of my castle, and the other is being pursued through my rear courtyard by Lord Rocambole. You'll be seeing him again soon enough."

"I can't wait."

The figure in black leapt down. As D stood beside his horse, there was the sound of the sword leaving the sheath on his back.

Feeling like this sound alone was enough to cut him, Gaskell drew his own longsword.

"Before we do this . . ." the general began, dropping the tip of his sword as he assumed a low position. His tone was strangely composed. "The way you got in here just now tells me something—it's actually quite a surprise, but it doesn't bother me *that* much. After the first time I met you, I think I must've realized it. However, there's something I don't understand. Why did the Sacred Ancestor order us to destroy you?"

A breathtakingly beautiful darkness spread over Gaskell's head—a darkness known as the man in black.

Gaskell barely managed to parry the silvery glint that came down from that darkness. The clang of steel meeting steel seemed to become a numbness that raced through every part of him. His head grew fuzzy.

Incredible! He really must be the Sacred Ancestor's own—

Without warning, the general was thrown off balance when D pulled away the sword that was locked against his. As the general staggered, the Hunter's blade streaked toward his waist. However, his prodigious form rose above the sword like some demonic bird, and he landed behind D. The great sword sped toward the Hunter's back in a slash aimed to cut him from the right side of his neck to the left armpit, but the blade was knocked back by a terrific impact accompanied by a shower of sparks. Without even turning, D had thrust his sword back over his shoulder to parry the blow.

Overcome for a moment by anger, the general brought his great sword back for a thrust instead. "Hyaaaah!" the general yelled as he made a lethal thrust that could pierce iron—and it did a perfect job of running D right through the neck. The instant Gaskell realized what he'd seen was only an afterimage left in empty space, the thrust D made with his own blade while falling backward jabbed cleanly into the left side of the great general's chest.

Though he trembled and was unable to speak, Gaskell made a giant leap away. Continuing on for a second bound, then a third, when he'd jumped over to a door to a corridor into his castle, he shouted, "Sorry, D. My heart's on the right side!"

Clots of blood spilled from his mouth.

Before D could kick off the ground again, the general shouldered his way through the passageway. The steel door closed, and a split second later a needle of rough wood bounced off its surface.

D didn't go after him. Turning around, he headed for the rear courtyard. There he should find Lord Rocambole and one of the two women.

III

With the unconscious Lady Ann over one shoulder, Lord Rocambole returned to the castle. The great general had told him where to find the other woman—Rosaria. Traversing a labyrinth of stairways and corridors, he finally came to a steel door, behind which Rosaria lay on a plush crimson bed. Brushing the hair from her face to compare it to Lady Ann's, Lord Rocambole donned a vicious grin. The vermilion lips unique to the Nobility gave a disturbing glimpse of white fangs.

"I see. Each is quite a beauty. At any rate, it would be a shame to take this girl's life just now. Perhaps I should wait for General Gaskell."

And saying this, the lord threw the girl down roughly, braced his sword against the floor, and leaned back against its hilt. His eyes shut—then opened again.

"An incredible presence is approaching," he murmured to no one in particular. "It's not Gaskell. Which would only leave . . . D. If he's going to be here soon, I shall have to arrange something to throw him off his game."

His eyes rested on Lady Ann, then shifted to Rosaria on the bed. Suddenly, he crinkled his brow.

"This woman . . ."

The way he said the words, they seemed to spill from someone else. Yet seemingly unable to be sure of something that filled his heart, his expression grew a bit more suspicious.

"Might you aid me in my battle against D?" he said, a devilish light in his eyes.

D stopped in the middle of the staircase. He sensed something was wrong. While he was certainly heading down, all five of his senses told him he hadn't advanced a single step.

"You've fallen into a maze," D's left hand informed him in a tone brimming with curiosity. "If you're not attuned to Gaskell's castle, you could keep going around and around on these stairs forever. Well, earth and fire will be too much trouble. What say we give it a try with just water and wind?"

It was unclear whether it was D or the source of that voice who put the Hunter's left hand out before him. A disturbing little face had surfaced in his palm. And it pursed its tiny, wrinkled lips.

Sticking out his right hand, D ran his left forefinger across its wrist. Although his fingernail didn't seem particularly long, the flesh split open and fresh blood dripped out. All of it fell into the left hand he'd positioned below—to be swallowed by that tiny maw. Continuing this for about three seconds, D then placed his left palm against the wound. There was a sucking sound, and the bleeding stopped.

Taking his left hand away, D raised it high above his head. From the vicinity of the palm there was a faint hiss of wind. In less than two seconds' time, it became the howling madness of a tempest.

The tiny mouth was sucking in air. And in the depths of that maw, a pale blue flame was rising.

D's eyes gave off blood light. Black hair rose, one strand banging against another like needles. A pair of trenchant fangs grew out of his gnashing teeth. The blood that flowed in his veins had been made manifest—D had turned into a true vampire.

"You know what you have to do, right?" the hoarse voice inquired.

There was no reply. All that escaped D's lips was a yell.

†

In an underground chamber, Lord Rocambole suddenly perked up his ears.

"Such a vicious cry. Such a powerful cry. Such a beautiful cry. And such a sad cry."

At his feet, Lady Ann said, "I know. I can hear it. It's a cry from my love. Which means he must be close." Perhaps the girl had wakened on hearing D's yell.

After speaking, Lady Ann stared intently at Lord Rocambole's face and said, "It can't be . . ."

There she broke off.

"Are you . . . crying?"

"Okay."

When the hoarse voice said this, D's cry halted. Like a gorgeous black statue on the brink of collapse, he swayed but did not fall. His trembling right hand reached over his shoulder for his longsword. Drawing the blade, D made a crude jab into the stairs beneath his feet. The stairway below him melted away like a swirling ammonite. D turned around—not a trace of the stairs remained behind him, either. The walls to either side had vanished, leaving him floating in the darkness on that one remaining step. A heartbeat later, he took to the air. There was no hesitation whatsoever. His coat spread like the wings of a mystic bird challenging a black abyss.

His body told him that zero time elapsed before the soles of his boots were back on solid ground.

D stood in a subterranean corridor. To his rear was the staircase.

How long had it been since he'd finished coming down those stairs?

A long cut from a sword remained clearly on the floor at his feet. To the right lay a dead end. D started down the corridor in the opposite direction. An iron door appeared. When he pushed against it, it creaked open.

There was no need to examine the situation. Rosaria lay on a crimson bed, and beside her an armored knight stood, as vigilant as a temple guardian. At his feet was Lady Ann, propping herself up with one arm.

"So glad you could come, D," Lord Rocambole said softly in greeting. There was something calm about his tone.

"You can't win like this," D said.

A weird and invisible aura gushed from every inch of the Hunter and assailed Rocambole. Rosaria shook from head to toe, and Lady Ann let out a little groan as she wrapped her arms around herself.

"I'll be damned," D's left hand moaned. For the instant the Hunter's unearthly aura had touched Rocambole, it'd disappeared completely. "I guess that's what you get with Gaskell's ultimate weapon. He's a real danger to you."

Given the distance between the two men, these whispered remarks from his hand shouldn't have traveled to the other's ears.

"That's right," Lord Rocambole said with a nod. "I've taken on the life force of three warriors. Even at that, I'm still only equal to you. But now, I shall claim another life. D, if you were me, which would *you* choose?"

His cape was closed in front of his chest, but a hand in black slipped out of it. In it, Rocambole held a longsword. The tip of it touched Lady Ann's left breast.

"Would it be this girl? Or—"

The blade moved darkly, pressing into the chest of Rosaria.

"—this woman? To tell the truth, I've already decided. Gaskell was brought back to life along with seven compatriots to help slay you—and I choose this girl, the last of them!"

Once again his blade jabbed at the swell of Lady Ann's bosom. Perhaps the reason Lady Ann didn't even look scared when he did so was because she was under the spell of Rocambole and the three lives he'd already claimed.

"Ordinarily, I would've taken this girl's life a long time ago. Do you know why I've waited, D?" Rocambole asked, and there was a strange emotion to his query. Under most circumstances, it would've been natural for his tone to be triumphant and mocking. Yet his question was perfectly serious.

D didn't answer.

Lord Rocambole continued, "I heard your voice earlier. It was beyond a doubt the voice of a Noble. It wasn't even that of a dhampir. An honest-to-goodness, full-blooded Noble—D, who are you? If your Noble blood is that strong, why are you out to get us? And another thing, D. Why have we each been given a new life to slay you now?"

His voice rang so mournfully that it nearly became a component of the darkness. By Providence, the person he put this query to would have to respond.

D's lips parted, allowing a voice like steel to escape. "I wouldn't call it a new life."

"What?"

"It may be a new destruction. Perhaps a permanent destruction."

Rocambole fell silent. Beneath his visor, there was a definite turbulence in his eyes. In the mere seconds it took for it to pass, he came to his conclusion.

"A new and permanent destruction. Could it be that we were—"

So despairing even his surprise had paled, Rocambole's tone made Lady Ann suddenly look up at him.

As he gazed up, his eyes met an enormous, towering stone statue. You might say it dominated the heavens, or that it was glowering down at the earth. Standing at its feet like a wrathful deity, the great General Gaskell had a strange glimmer in his eyes as he looked up at the distant stony visage.

"The new life you've given me, Sacred Ancestor, seems likely to meet the unhappiest of ends."

From this statement, it was clear the statue depicted the Sacred Ancestor. Why would the great General Gaskell—a man who'd opposed him and proved the worst traitor in history—have a statue of the Sacred Ancestor in his own castle?

One look at the statue made the reason clear. The dignity that radiated from the ordinary stone figure overwhelmed all who beheld it, searing their minds with an unmistakable sense of terror. Having fought him once, it wasn't surprising that General Gaskell kept the statue of his sworn foe in a room in his castle known only to himself.

"Six of the original seven have been slain, and only Rocambole and the girl remain," Gaskell continued. There was something defiant about his tone, but a hint of sadness crept into it. "Once he's taken the girl's life, chances are very good that he shall triumph. That was the mission you gave us. It was carved into the stone tablet I have no recollection of placing in the hands of this statue I crafted of you. And along with that order were the names of seven assassins. The last name alone was so weathered I couldn't make it out, but it must've been the daughter of the Duke of Xenon—"

The statue of the Sacred Ancestor still held a stone tablet. On it were carved seven names that were now worn into illegibility.

"All I had to do was assemble the seven of them. Their brains, too, had been impressed with the order to slay D, like a brand that wouldn't fade for all eternity. However, six of them have been destroyed, and I myself have been grievously injured. Surely it wouldn't have been impossible for someone with the Sacred Ancestor's power to give them strength surpassing D's. After five were slain, I noticed the truth, and at the same time I was captivated by a hair-raising conjecture. Sacred Ancestor! Could it be that's what was intended for us? No, it couldn't be—yet it seems to be the case. Not even the Sacred Ancestor would do something like that . . . We were merely assembled to slay D. If not, there's no point in even trying to destroy him."

From Gaskell's hip, a streak of black lightning ran in reverse. Gaskell waved the sword he'd drawn at the stone statue as if threatening it.

"Such must be the case, O Sacred Ancestor. State it plainly. Tell me we were resurrected to slay D, not reborn to be slain by him. No, I shall prove as much soon enough—once Rocambole has carved out D's heart and lopped off his head. The man has gained three lives. Not even D is a match for him. By now, he'll have taken the last—absorbed a fourth life—and become a fearsome, invincible swordsman."

At some point, his tone had become desperate. Was this the voice of one of the generals feared as the most ferocious in history?

He kept his silence for a moment before crying, "Sacred Ancestor!" His words were nearly a prayer.

Above him, he sensed a movement. Looking up, Gaskell gasped.

The statue's hand came down, its worn fingers still tightly grasping the stone slate. As if to say, *Read it.*

Sword of Devastation

CHAPTER 7

I

It was said that in regions where one of the Nobility's castles remained, whether there were still Nobles in it or not, the darkness was that much deeper. On one of their few festival days, the dancing people would be terrified to see lights burning in a castle's windows, telling them their revelry was at an end—they inspired such fear. One theory was that on the nights when Greater Nobles were troubled, the darkness would split itself open, sink teeth into itself, and let flow an even denser darkness as its blood. If so, the darkness that surrounded Castle Gaskell this night was unbelievably thick.

A certain notion had turned a fearsome Noble into a tortured ghost. He'd already asked himself this question: *Why am I here?*

"D!" he called out to his foe. "D, if you know, please tell me. Were we brought back to life not to slay you, but rather to be slain by you?"

The air suddenly froze solid. D didn't answer. However, the whole world knew. Rocambole knew. So did Lady Ann. Even the still-slumbering Rosaria knew the reply.

That's it exactly.

"It's just as I thought, then," Rocambole said with a nod. "Earlier, while I was waiting for you, it suddenly came to me. What did all of us who were called back from the long sleep of death have in common? Our skill in combat? No, there were others who were our equals. It seemed the seven of us were completely separate, without any connection—except where you were concerned, that is. And that made me think. Gaskell brought us back, but he was revived and bidden to call us together by the Sacred Ancestor. What was similar about our relationship to the Sacred Ancestor? That required no thought at all. In life, each and every one of us rebelled against him. And it goes without saying that General Gaskell was the very worst in that respect. He, too, was destined for destruction but was brought back to life. So far, my theory holds water, D."

Rocambole's eyes were crazed with a horrible despair. He bent backward and laughed, and his howls were so fiendish that Lady Ann covered her ears in spite of herself.

"Living to be destroyed? Okay, so be it. If that's the will of the Sacred Ancestor, any resistance is useless. But, useless or not, resistance is resistance. And the one who offers it, even if he's no better than a bug, must make his will known. D, I may be destroyed, but I won't let you leave here alive. Or the girl you came here to save."

Lord Rocambole's sword rose and pointed to Rosaria, still lying on the bed.

"Wait!" Lady Ann shouted, and, seeing that she hadn't stayed Rocambole's hand, she continued, "That woman—by all means, allow me to kill her."

"Oh, what's this?" D's left hand murmured, but apparently no one noticed; nor did the group seem to show any surprise at Lady Ann's sudden request. The girl had a blind love of D—and in light of this, her reaction was considered perfectly natural.

"D—are you determined to save this woman at any cost?" the girl cried out, waving one arm in Rosaria's direction after desperately struggling to her feet. "By my oath, that woman doesn't love you in the least. In all the world, no one loves you but I. And yet you would forsake me and save her, so I'm going to finish her here and now. D, I don't ask you to say that you care for me. However, you could've at least chosen me over her. Now you can stand there and watch as I kill her."

Lady Ann's cries were dripping with malice and grief. Her sweet little hand rose to her lips, caught a red rose, and came away again.

"Put this through her chest—"

Ah, what would happen if one of the same lethal blooms that had brought Grand Duke Mehmet, Dr. Gretchen, and the Dark One, Major General Gillis, all to the brink of death were to be stuck into an ordinary human?

"—and within two seconds, she'll be a mummy. Watch this, Lord Rocambole."

The girl raised the hand that held the rose she'd disgorged and prepared to hurl it toward the bed. A white needle pierced the flower, only stopping when it sank into the stone wall. A second after it was pierced, the rose fell to pieces, with Lady Ann staring down absentmindedly at the two petals resting in her hand.

"Oh, you truly aren't the sort of man to be moved by a woman's feelings," she said, eyes like black gemstones filling with tears. "In that case, I shall have to be as insistent about taking this woman's life as you are about saving it."

She brought her other hand to her lips, and then raised it even higher with a crimson rose in its grip. The rough wooden needle that came flying at it was batted down by Rocambole's longsword. But a red flower suddenly bloomed in the Nobleman's right eye.

What was all this? He bent backward without saying anything.

Having leapt up beside him, Lady Ann scooped Rosaria up in her slender arms and threw her toward D. But by catching the woman, D was unable to halt Rocambole's next move.

Fighting through the pain of being stabbed through one eye, the lord let the longsword in his right hand streak into action. The arc of his blade passed through the nape of Lady Ann's neck just as she was about to land. No fresh blood shot out, but her slim neck was half severed, and the girl slumped to the floor and moved no more. Even while she was falling, Rocambole tried to extract the crimson flower that had blossomed in his right eye with one hand.

"Do the roots go down to the very bone?" he groaned before finally giving up. From the center of that red bloom, something redder still had begun to drip.

Laying Rosaria on the floor, D calmly straightened up again. Out of the corner of his eye, he could see Lady Ann lying there like a doll.

"Three people's lives," was all D said.

Was the Hunter asking if that was enough to beat him? That was the way Rocambole interpreted it.

"More than enough!"

He ran. As did D. Two black silhouettes melted into one—then pulled apart. Part of the silhouette spread as if shredded by the wind, blooming into a massive bloody flower. Actually, there were *two* flowers—their steely blades had shot out simultaneously to tear open each other's flank, in precisely the same spot, to exactly the same depth.

Clutching their wounds, the two men spun around.

"Oh, that dirty dog stole your trick—it looks like he can mimic anyone's abilities in a split second," said the hoarse voice.

D understood this, too.

"What do you think, D?" Rocambole asked, giving his longsword a shake. "I still have two lives left. Three, if you count my own—meaning I can die three more times. In order to stop me, you shall have to slay me. However, I'll also be able to draw on whatever techniques you use to do so. The question is, will you live long enough to kill me three more times?"

D stuck his left hand out in front of himself.

"What's this?" Rocambole said, but no sooner had he narrowed his eyes suspiciously than the Hunter lopped his own left hand off with a single stroke.

"What are you—hey!" the hoarse voice exclaimed.

"If I'm slain, you're to do nothing for me and leave," D commanded. His quiet tone carried an iron will.

After a few moments had passed, the hoarse voice responded from somewhere on the floor, "I get you."

Doing nothing to stanch the flow of blood from his left wrist, D said, "You can die three times—I can die once. That should do."

Even though Rocambole had taken on three more lives, as long as D had the energy generator that was his left hand, the lord had no chance of victory. But why would D deny himself that advantage?

The murderous intent faded from Rocambole's good eye. "I'm not exactly sure, but I suppose I should probably thank you for doing that," he said. "But I won't be destroyed. That would be an insult to all those who lost their lives against you, as well as those whose lives I received."

A new fire burned in his good eye. It wasn't malice that resided there, but rather an amazingly pure fervor for battle. However, it was unclear whether he realized his words were almost exactly the same as Grand Duke Mehmet's when he had faced Rocambole. The flow of blood from the flower in his right eye suddenly grew more intense.

They ran at the same time—both leaving the same distance behind them, both tracing the same path with their swords. The sparks were red as the weapons clanged together, and the tips of both were equally sharp as they bit into the opponent's shoulder.

As the two staggered away from each other they were a frightening sight. If D was the very picture of horror, with blood gushing not only from the wounds to the left nape of his neck and his side but also from where he'd taken off his own left hand, then Lord Rocambole was every bit as shocking with those same neck and side wounds, plus the endless trickle of blood from the ensanguined flower that bloomed in his right eye socket.

Three deaths versus one—but regardless of those numbers, the next attack would decide this battle. The heavens knew as much. The earth knew, too.

Seeing D return his sword to its sheath, Lord Rocambole grew tense. However, no matter what kind of swordplay the Hunter might try, the lord's ability would allow him to duplicate it. Self-confidence put a smile on his lips.

D kicked off the ground. Silently, easily—and powerfully. Rocambole did the same.

A third time they would clash—but just before they did, D doubled over. Feeling coldness from the blade that slipped so naturally from the Hunter's sheath, Rocambole deflected it with a gleaming stroke from his longsword.

D made a great twist to the right. His chest was fully exposed. Rocambole's body was right in the path of the Hunter's blade.

Rocambole heard a voice somewhere shout, *Don't!*

A second before he was impaled, D twisted his body a little more to the right, and Rocambole froze with the realization that he'd missed the vital spot, while above the lord's head the sword he'd batted away, which had barely remained in D's grasp, now came straight down in a blow that was like someone splitting firewood—ripping through him from the top of his head down to his crotch in a single motion.

Not even D himself knew what effect his unpredictable attack was going to have, so Lord Rocambole hadn't been able to use his ability to duplicate it.

As Rocambole split in two, suit of armor and all, D fell again to one knee beside him. Rocambole's sword had come out through his back. Grabbing its hilt, D extracted the weapon. His breaths were short and shallow. Something superhuman—and something other than sheer will—let D rise to his feet again. Covered in blood from head to toe, he called to mind some exquisite wraith.

When he went down on one knee again, it was by Lady Ann's side. Still, that seemed enough to put some life back into the girl's pallid visage. Eyes that had been shut now opened wide, and she said in a wistful tone, "D—"

"Rosaria is okay," D told her. "Thanks to you."

"Good," Lady Ann said with a smile. "I'm glad—but are you crying?"

D shook his head.

"I didn't think so. That's why you just won't die."

It seemed like the girl didn't even know what death was.

Gazing at D, she said, "You have nothing to say to the dying, do you? Is that how you were raised?"

"I suppose."

"It would probably pain Father to have such a man watching over me as I go." A mournful shadow skimmed across her blossomlike expression. "But there's nothing to be done about that. I managed to help the woman you were so determined to save. That's enough for me."

Her eyelids soon drooped.

"I don't know when it'll be, but when you get to where I'm going, might we dwell in the same kingdom?"

D nodded. On noticing that Lady Ann had shut her eyes completely, D said, "Yes," but by that time a change had begun in Lady Ann's body.

Several seconds later, D was looking down at a wooden doll that lay at his feet. It must've been carved by a craftsman beloved of the gods. The face and body still retained the likeness of the girl who'd been known as Lady Ann.

A faint sound made D turn around.

Apparently Rocambole wasn't the type to go gentle into that good night. Using his left hand to hold together his vertically bisected body, the longsword he held between his lips quivered as he used his right hand to drag his bloodied form toward Lady Ann.

II

"Just . . . one . . . more."

These words spilled from the lord's barely parted lips. The steely fingers rose from the stone floor, scratched feebly across its surface, and rose again, this time managing to pull him about a foot across the floor.

"If I had . . . one more life . . . I could . . . slay D."

But as he said this, he wasn't looking at D. There was some question as to whether he could see anything at all. The only thing that drove Lord Rocambole onward was a crazed obsession.

Behind him, someone said, "No, this can't be."

"This can't be!"

As General Gaskell cried out, his eyes bulged, for he'd read the letters on the stone slate. And he'd been able to distinguish on its surface the seventh name that until ten seconds or so ago had been worn away into illegibility.

Baron Schuma
Madame Laurencin
Grand Duke Mehmet
Roland, the Duke of Xenon
Dr. Gretchen
Lord Rocambole

And—

Turning with unbelievable strength, Lord Rocambole opened his dead fish eyes wide.

The great General Gaskell called out the seventh name.
Rosaria.

The woman who rose so mysteriously from the floor now had the form of Rosaria, without a doubt. However, D of all people wouldn't call out to her. The bloody hue of her eyes told him that the reason the woman had awakened was to destroy him.

"So, you finally caught up to me. The *real* me."

As she said this, a beastly pair of fangs poked from between her lips.

"You're the seventh?" D asked.

"Yes. But I only realized it just now. Those were the days, D. I miss the girl I was when I was traveling with you."

Rosaria shifted her gaze to Lord Rocambole, still lying on the floor. "If you'd killed me to begin with, you might've slain D," she said.

"There's still . . . time . . . Kill . . . D!"

Rocambole's sheer will to live must've been nearly exhausted, because the vermilion line running through him was growing broader. No doubt the words that spilled from him with that bloody foam were part of his last gasp.

"Pleasant dreams, Lord Rocambole."

"Damn you . . . You've betrayed . . . all of us . . ."

Before he'd even finished speaking, his body split in two again. Even his fearsome Noble vitality had reached its limit.

Rosaria looked down at his remains for a few seconds, and then walked toward the door. Without even turning around, she said, "I'm going to find Gaskell."

When D started to follow her, a hoarse voice called out, "Hey, wait for me!"

D held his left arm out in its direction, and the hand whistled through the air and reattached itself to his wrist.

"That's a convenient accessory you have," Rosaria remarked coolly.

"What are you talking about? I'm an independent—" the hoarse voice started to squawk, but one clench of D's fist silenced it as the Hunter followed Rosaria through the doorway.

"So, the Hunter and the traitor are coming?" General Gaskell mused with a nod, his eyes closed as he stood in the room that housed the great stone statue. Though there wasn't a single monitor screen there, apparently his shut eyes were viewing something.

"So be it."

He opened his eyes. They held a ferocious glint of determination.

Turning his face up a bit, he said in a voice that was like a rumbling in the earth, "Destroy the castle. Have it completely disappear fifteen minutes from now. And cancel all the abort sequences."

"Affirmative. Your commands will be carried out," a mechanical voice responded from nowhere in particular.

"I wish you luck, D!"

A white light that radiated from the ceiling enveloped General Gaskell's body. A second later, he was on the rooftop of the castle. Ahead and to the left rested an object that looked like a misshapen globe entangled in a trio of cylinders. An aircraft for escape purposes, it was usually stored on the floor below. Walking over to it with broad strides, Gaskell was about to climb in through the hatch that opened automatically, but then he felt something cold creep down his neck.

The general turned around. Before him, a pair of silhouettes basked in the moonlight.

"Oh, and just how did you get here?" Gaskell must've realized that his plan to escape had been foiled, because his voice swelled with an impressive resolve.

"Actually, I'm one of the assassins you selected. So I'm in sync with this castle," Rosaria replied matter-of-factly.

Standing beside her, D had become a vision of beauty.

"I see. Meaning that anything I can do, you can also do? And I'm the one who made it that way." Staring intently at D, he said, "I understand why this Hunter would come after me. But why you? Have you forgotten your mission as an assassin?"

"I was given the task of making D lower his guard so that I might slay him. Perhaps it was because my approach was different from all the rest, but the will of a certain great man remained in my head. General—I'm sure you probably realize as much already, but we were all born to be *slain* by D."

"I know that. Now," the general replied. "The timing of my resurrection, my calling you all together for what I thought was D's destruction, and even D coming here—all these things were determined long ago by a majestic will. Do you realize that?"

The general's gaze bored through the gorgeous Hunter.

"People are waiting for me," D said softly, as if all of what Gaskell had said was merely an illusion.

"Hmm—then the truth of this doesn't matter to you? You frighten me. Your mind does. Can you understand that, D? It's because you remind me of a certain great man."

An astonished face turned to look at D—that of Rosaria.

"It can't be—there was nothing about that in my memories, but . . . D, are you . . ."

"That's right, Rosaria. It wasn't I that guided you toward this destiny. Long ago, a certain eminent personage laid it all out. Surely you realize by now who that was, don't you? And what his relationship is to this Hunter," the general laughed wickedly. "So, whom will you bare those fangs against? D, or me? Give this careful consideration. You and I—together, the two of us are more than D could handle at one time."

Rosaria was gazing at D. A weird kind of miasma had begun to rise from her body.

His grin broadening, the great General Gaskell drew his sword.

"D," Rosaria said, tears gleaming in her eyes, "I really enjoyed traveling with you."

A cloud of miasma sailed straight up from every inch of the woman. In midair it took on an enormous, beastly form, with a tail streaming behind it like a comet as it streaked into battle—against General Gaskell!

"What idiocy is this?" he shouted, the tip of his black steel slipping through the beast's white back.

Lifeblood spread like ink in the moonlight.

General Gaskell staggered as he held the nape of his own neck.

The beast bounded to a spot a good fifteen feet away. Its body like a mass of fog, the creature didn't have a mark on it. On the first night the woman had met D, it was this beast that had destroyed everyone in the valley of victims.

"I'm done taking my revenge," Rosaria announced coolly. But was that statement for the general's benefit? Or for D's?

"And now I must complete my mission. D—no matter what kind of attack you use against this beast, it won't die. And there's nothing else I can do. Slaying you is—"

Without warning, Rosaria turned her gaze to the castle wall. She couldn't see down it. However, it seemed she'd glimpsed something anyway. The smile that graced her lips was terribly warm.

"Those three transporters—it looks like they got here after all. They had to come see you, didn't they?"

"No, to see *you*," D said softly.

"They're such sweet guys. The most fun I ever had was the time I spent being human." Suddenly crinkling her brow, she continued, "But I wonder how on earth they ever got through the gates."

The blue pendant on D's chest gave off a delicate glow.

"Why don't you say hello to them?"

Rosaria stared at D as if stunned. Something glistened in her eyes.

Walking over to the stone wall, she peered down. Not long thereafter, a voice was heard to say, "Look—it's Rosaria!"

"Sergei!" the woman exclaimed.

D nodded ever so slightly.

"You're still okay? Excellent!"

"And Juke," she said.

"We're coming. Hold on!"

"That's Gordo's voice," Rosaria remarked, waving one hand.

A cheer of *Yeah!* went up. *Just hold on!*

Rosaria went back to where she'd been. Something glittered its way down her cheeks.

"I don't want those guys to see any of this. I don't want them to see me . . . D."

And as she said this, her teary eyes gave off a blood light, and the air of insanity around her vicious beast swelled as it pounced.

D's longsword went into action.

The Hunter put pressure on his shoulder, and blood that looked like wine trickled out from between his fingers.

When the beast landed about fifteen feet away, there was no sign of a wound on it.

"Not even you . . . can defeat that beast . . ." said the great General Gaskell, who was soaked in blood as he slumped back into his aircraft. "If you're going to deal the coup de grâce, Rosaria, you'd better hurry. This castle has less than five minutes remaining until it disappears."

There was turbulence in Rosaria's eyes as she focused them on the castle wall. Was she concerned for the transporter trio?

A second later, D leapt. The beast counterattacked. Both blade and talons were brandished in midair.

At that moment, something happened. Rosaria looked up to the sky in amazement, and even General Gaskell bugged his eyes.

Had D really done *that*?

The beast ripped open diagonally. Like a common cur, it yelped in its death throes and dissolved in midair.

At the same time, Rosaria also fell. The instant she did, her body split along a diagonal line. D alone could see that the angle and placement of the cut were exactly the same as the wound he'd dealt the beast.

"Wha—what the hell did you do?"

Even though D recognized the voice that rang out behind him, he didn't turn around.

The first one over the castle wall had been Gordo. Juke and Sergei were just poking their heads up now. Grappling hooks were snagged on the castle walls—they'd used the ropes attached to them to make their ascent. Because each rope gun was equipped with a winch, it could haul its owner all the way to the top.

"I saw everything. How could you do that to Rosaria?"

Anger had stained Gordo's brain with madness. Needless to say, he hadn't actually watched D cut down Rosaria—what Gordo saw was Rosaria fall and split in two. Based on her location, it couldn't have been Gaskell. So, that only left one person. Gordo didn't think, *No, D could never do that.* He was prejudiced against dhampirs. Besides, anything could happen out here. This was the Frontier.

Drawing the machete from his hip, Gordo charged forward.

"G-Gordo!"

By the time Juke and Sergei had jumped down onto the roof from the top of the wall, their compatriot was running at D's back with his machete poised waist high. D made no effort to dodge it, and Gordo's machete sank into the figure in black all the way to the handle. The end of it poked from the Hunter's abdomen.

Ahead of D, the aircraft rose. There was nothing the seriously wounded D could do about it as it climbed, then flew off to the west.

"Another day, I guess," D said, looking up at the constellations, and then he turned back to Gordo. The most unruly of the transporters had been pinned to the ground by Juke and Sergei.

"You idiot!"

"How could you be so stupid?"

Ignoring them as they kicked and punched the third man, D walked over to Rosaria.

"Was she under some kind of spell?" Juke asked.

"Yes," D replied. Of course, he didn't tell them that she'd been a Noble from the very start.

"Two minutes," the hoarse voice told them. "The castle will be destroyed in two minutes—so run for it!"

"We can't just leave Rosaria here," said Sergei.

"Come on," D said, reaching out and grabbing Juke with one arm and Sergei with the other.

"Hey, what am I supposed to do?" Gordo pleaded.

"Grab on," D replied, already headed for the castle wall.

"Shit!" the man cried, running over and grabbing D around the neck.

A second later, the four of them were in the air. There was no saying how long it was before they landed. Nor did they know why there'd been no shock on impact.

The castle collapsed as if it were made of sand. Blasted by the minute particles, the three humans had to shut their eyes tight and turn away—unlike D.

"Can you use a blade now?" D inquired once the storm of sandy grit had abated.

As Juke and Sergei watched him, Gordo looked down at his hands, his eyes open wide.

"No problem—it's like, when I stabbed you . . ."

"That was a present from Rosaria," D said.

The reason was obvious.

Still holding the same pose, Gordo dropped to his knees. Tears streamed down his wildly bearded face.

It was a week later that the group's journey came to an end. After bringing their merchandise to the last village, the three transporters bid farewell to D at the edge of town.

"If we're ever in trouble again, come bail us out," Juke said, offering his right hand.

Saying nothing, D gripped it. No one was surprised—it seemed perfectly natural to all of them.

"We'll be waiting for you as long as we live," Gordo said, with a clap on D's shoulder.

"Hell, we don't need you," Sergei said, shooting him a grin. "My smarts will be enough to save us all."

D remained silent as he wheeled his steed around. The trio headed back down the road that had brought them there. D was headed forward, as always.

"Gaskell got away. He'll be back again," a voice from the vicinity of D's left hand said after some time had passed. "But even if all seven disobeyed the Sacred Ancestor, I wonder why he'd go to all the trouble of having you destroy them at this late date? Sacred Ancestor or not, I guess he couldn't prevent them from entering that sleep. His laws are ironclad, and there's no point in them even rebelling against the Sacred Ancestor again. Hmm."

The hoarse voice was neither posing a question nor seeking D's agreement. It knew it would never get an answer out of him.

"Oh, look at the sky—those are thunderheads!"

Before the voice had finished speaking, a shadow moved across the sun, and thunder echoed in the distance.

"Even nature is against you—you must have some really bad karma!"

D rode forward without saying a word. His elegantly beautiful countenance suggested that not a single memory remained of those two women and three men.

END

Postscript

The only reason I agreed to appear in a TV program was because I thought, "If I'm on TV, it'll probably help make me famous." However, I'm not the most social of people, so it was going to be taxing to spend twenty days with the ten or so people involved (and due to a certain mishap, the time ended up stretching to twenty-five days). The trip itself was interesting. It consisted of Bran Castle (which remains for sale at present); the ruins of Targoviste Castle, where Vlad Tepes spent his youth; and Castle Dracula, towering up on the mountaintop. What surprised me during my second visit was that in front of the bridge leading to the castle, there was a little old man from a nearby village who was reading a newspaper, and he charged us admission. I suppose this is one of the effects of liberalization in Romania. The size of the wad of tickets he was carrying made quite an impression on me. In the castle's garden were the remains of a bonfire started by tourists. To be honest, the structure seems a little too small to be called a castle. What we see in Coppola's *Dracula* is far too grand. I suppose it'd be better to call it a *fort* rather than a *castle*. Movie or not, that anyone would transform it into such a mountain stronghold just goes to show what a master of embellishment *Dracula* author Bram Stoker must've been. (*Laughs*)

Speaking of Stoker's embellishments, in the original novel and subsequent films, the scene where Jonathan Harker changes coaches at the Borgo Pass is unsettling, while in fact the place is a fairly gentle stretch of land that opens up after you've climbed a little bit. Couples were sunbathing at the very top of the pass, while to the right loomed what was, all appearances to the contrary, "Hotel Castel Dracula." Naturally that's where we stayed. I lay down in a coffin on display there, and they filmed me getting up out of it. Oh, it really was cramped in there.

It was from Romania's neighbor Bulgaria and the port town of Varna that Dracula headed to London by ship. Though we went there, it was cut out of the finished broadcast. When we got up in the morning, fog made it impossible to see down the streets, which was quite fun. Well, seeing how Dracula was living out in the sticks with three wives who didn't do a lick of housework and had no talent except for drinking blood, it comes as little surprise that he'd want to relocate to someplace lively like a major city. And when the ship pulled out of that port (supposing it was at night), I can picture Dracula shouting back to the brides he left behind, "See you, suckers!"

Finally, I'd like to end this with an experience that was more hair raising than an encounter with a vampire. When we were returning to Paris from Bucharest, there was a French TV crew with us, but when we arrived and were relaxing at a café, we suddenly heard an incredible explosion. Startled, we looked all around, but everyone else was perfectly calm. At that point, one of our cameramen, who'd gone off to the Lost and Found, came back and told us that apparently there'd been a bomb in someone's luggage. When he went to check out the scene, there was video tape scattered everywhere. It seems the bomb had probably been in the other TV crew's bags. But my blood ran cold at the thought of what would've happened if it had gone off while we were in the air.

Hideyuki Kikuchi
March 16, 2010
while watching *Dracula* (Royal Winnipeg Ballet)

And now, a preview of the next book in the
Vampire Hunter D series

VAMPIRE HUNTER D

VOLUME 16

TYRANT'S STARS PARTS ONE AND TWO

Written by
Hideyuki Kikuchi

Illustrations by
Yoshitaka Amano

English translation by
Kevin Leahy

Coming in December 2010
from Dark Horse Books and Digital Manga Publishing

The Coming of an Evil Star

I

Eyes shut, he sat on his throne listening to the sounds of battle ringing out on the floor below. He shouldn't have been hearing these sounds. The clang of sword on sword as iron met steel, the scream of severed flesh and bone, and then the sounds that took their place—the thud of combatants hitting the floor without so much as a final cry. He could even see the sparks that resulted when blade struck blade. All the defensive systems of his castle had been rendered ineffective and his warriors had been slain, and all that remained were the last fifteen stalwart individuals who now faced his fearsome foe in the chamber beneath him.

There was no light in his room. Naturally, there were no windows, either. Though there were those who, despite having eyes that could see in complete darkness, used candles, lamps, and other sources of light just as humans did, he had forgone all of that. As a result, there was nothing in this room except the chair on which he sat, a table, and a coffin. He had no need of the darkness outside. So long as he remained in this room, an inky blackness equally dark and dense would surround him forever.

How long had it been since he'd decided not to leave this room?

A white glow shone behind his eyelids: someone's face. He heard an agonized cry. The groan that rang out was the death rattle of the fifteenth of his retainers, stabbed through the heart.

It was too early. Amazing, even impossible—such speed was terrifying. His foe was truly capable. There was a feverish aching deep in his chest. Power called to power—but though he endeavored to recall the person's name, he fared poorly. That had all been forgotten long ago, the instant he took a seat in this room. And ever since, he'd been at peace.

Inaudible footsteps were climbing the stairs. Unable to slow the racing of his heart, he opened his eyes. Dust filled his field of view, but the world soon became visible.

His foe was on the other side of the door. The dimensional vortex, phase-switching device, hypnocircuits, and other defenses that had been imprinted into the two-inch-thick door would no doubt do their deadly best to eliminate the intruder. But he got the feeling none of them would do any good. His brain could no longer form any picture from the sounds he heard. But between the door and that attacker, a breathtaking life-or-death conflict had to be taking place.

A minute passed.

There was a flash at one edge of the door—at the side where the lock was. It carved the lock right out of the door as if it were slicing through water.

The door was opening without a sound. And he was directly across from it. The fine crack of light grew broader, and when it'd taken on an oblong shape, he saw the shadowy figure who stood on the other side. In the intruder's right hand was the sword he'd lowered. Oddly enough, not a single drop of blood clung to its blade. He wore a wide-brimmed traveler's hat and a black, long coat. The instant the Nobleman glimpsed the face below that hat, he let a gasp of surprise escape in spite of himself. He had to clear his throat with a cough before he could even speak.

"I'd heard there was a Hunter of unearthly beauty out there, but I never thought I'd lay eyes on him myself. I am Count Braujou. And you are?"

"D."

His reply was more a concept than a word.

"That's what I'd heard."

First his eyelids and now his lips—both had caused storms of swirling dust, but through it Count Braujou stared at the gorgeous embodiment of death who stood there, silent and stock still.

"I didn't think there was anyone left in the world who'd hire you to destroy me. The outside world should've long since forgotten about my manse, my servants, and me. Why, when I stepped into this room for the last time, it must've been—"

"Five thousand and one years ago," said the assassin who'd identified himself as D, supplying the answer. The way he spoke without a whit of murderous intent, Count Braujou couldn't help but voice his surprise.

"Hmm, has it been that long? So, is it the farmers of this region who've come to find an old fossil of a Noble like me an obstruction? I don't suppose a Hunter like yourself is too free with information, but if you could, I'd like you to tell me who sent you."

"It's the Capital," D said.

"The Capital? But these are the southernmost reaches of the southern Frontier—not the kind of place likely to draw the least bit of attention from the Capital."

"For human beings, five millennia is time enough for a great many things to change," said D. "The Capital has set about actively developing the Frontier regions. On the surface, it appears that they're out to eliminate the abhorrent influence of the Nobility who remain on the Frontier—and give the farmers some peace of mind— but their actual aim is the things hidden in places like this."

The count smiled thinly.

"The wisdom and treasures of the Nobility? So, the lowly humans would pick through the dregs of those they called monsters? I can see where a fossil like me might be a hindrance."

He made a bow to D where he stood by the door.

"Thank you for sharing this with me. I greatly appreciate it. And to show my gratitude, I shall shake off five millennia of rust and battle you with all my heart and soul."

Putting his hands on the armrests, the count slowly rose to his feet. From head to foot he was shrouded in gray detritus—dust that had collected on him over the span of five thousand years. Since taking his place in that chair, he hadn't moved a single step. The dust actually felt rather nice as it slid off his skin.

Putting his hands on his hips, the count stretched. Not only from his waist, but also from his spine and shoulder blades there were snaps and pops. Warming himself up, he swung his arms from side to side, bending and stretching them.

"It seems I'm not as rusty as I thought. I suppose this place will serve."

Looking around, he found the entire chamber filled with ash gray. The eddying dust constantly filled his field of view.

All this time, D watched him silently. You might say it was an incredible folly on his part. Who in their right mind would give a motionless Noble the chance to move again?

The count reached for the spear that was leaning against his chair. Once he'd grabbed it and given it a single swing, the dust fell from it, and his imposing black weapon was awakened from five thousand years of sleep. Twenty feet long, the great spear had a tip that ran a third of that length, and although it seemed like it would be a highly impractical toy or decoration, such would be the case only if this weapon were in the hands of an ordinary person. Having risen from his throne, the Nobleman stood exactly ten feet tall—it was over six and a half feet from the floor to the seat of his chair. Yet the way he pointed his weapon at D's chest without another test swing or any rousing battle cry seemed terribly simplistic, and the count was entirely devoid of killing lust. Just like D.

"Most kind of you to wait. Have at you!" he said, and then the entire situation changed.

D's body warped as if he were behind a heat shimmer. The murderous intent radiating from the tip of the Nobleman's spear was transforming the air. A normal adversary would've fainted dead away just by seeing it directed at him.

In response, D slowly raised his longsword.

Just then, the count said, "My word—who knew that D was such a man?" This time his voice shook with infinite terror as the words spilled from the corner of his mouth. But whatever he'd felt, it would never be made known.

D kicked off the floor. Only those Nobles who'd fallen to his blade knew how amazing and horrifying it was to have it come down at their heads. A millisecond opening—and then a glittering waterwheel spun beneath that shooting star and the trail it left behind. Was it sparks that were sent flying, or the blade?

With the most mellifluous of sounds, D's sword bounced back, and the hem of his black garb spread like the wings of some mystic bird as he made a great bound to the left. As the Hunter landed, so gentle he didn't stir up even a mote of dust, the head of the spinning spear whistled toward his feet. The figure in black narrowly evaded it with a leap, but the shaft of the weapon buzzed at his torso from an impossible angle, only to meet his sword with a thud.

The swipe D made with his blade in midair was something to be feared. Because a heartbeat later, the spear's apparently steel shaft had been severed a foot and a half from the end and was sailing through the air. D's left hand then rose, and a black glint screamed through the air to pierce the base of the giant's throat with unerring accuracy.

Though he staggered for an instant without making a sound, Count Braujou swiftly grabbed the murderous implement with his left hand and tossed it away, groaning, "What have we here?"

It was the severed end of the spear. Lopping it off, D had caught it with his left hand and hurled it like a throwing knife. And that was probably the reason why he'd sliced it off at an angle.

However, even as black blood gushed from the wound, the giant wasn't the least bit rattled as he stood with his long spear at the ready.

And D was equally composed. The right ankle of his boot was split diagonally with fresh blood seeping out, making it known that the count's attack earlier hadn't been without effect, yet the Hunter remained perfectly still with his sword out straight at eye level like an exquisite ice sculpture standing in the inky blackness.

The darkness solidified. The temperature in the room was rapidly falling, thanks to the killing lust that billowed at D from the giant.

What would D do to counter that?

The young man in black simply stood there. In fact, the killing lust disappeared as soon as it touched him—it was unclear whether he absorbed it or deflected it. However, his form distorted mysteriously, and from it there was just one flash—his blade alone remaining immutable, poised to take action against the fearsome spear man.

There was no point in asking which of them moved. Harsh sparks were scattered in a chamber lacquered over with five millennia of pitch blackness.

But before their transient light vanished in the air, a voice told the Hunter, "Wait. The life I abandoned five millennia ago isn't dear to me. I have remained here like the dead for just such a moment as this. D—we will settle this. But may I ask that before I fulfill this promise to you, you allow me to fulfill an earlier pledge?"

The murderous intent had already evaporated, and the two figures—one with sword extended, the other with long spear sweeping to one side—looked as if they might've dissolved into one.

"A star just shot by," D said.

His head only came up to about the solar plexus of the giant. But from a room with no windows, his eyes had apparently glimpsed something in space.

"Is that the reason?"

"Valcua has returned," the giant said.

There was a faraway sound to his voice, and a distant look in his eyes. Those same eyes gave off a red glow.

"And he's bound to see to it that those who drove him into space are charred to the bone. He'll be merciless with their innocent descendants. But I must prevent him from doing so. For you see, it's in keeping with a pledge I made in days long past to one of their ancestors."

The tangled silhouettes separated. At the same time the count lowered his long spear there was the click of hilt against scabbard by D's shoulder. His blade had been sheathed. Turning a defenseless back to his foe, D walked toward the door.

"You have my thanks," the count said, although it was unclear if his words reached the Hunter. "The last time I raise my spear, it shall be against you."

As D exited the darkened chamber, his left hand rose casually, and from it a hoarse voice said, "I really have to hand it to you this time. You saw it. I did, too. Yep, we saw the same thing he did. A wicked star fell in the northern reaches. I can still see the long, long tail that streamed behind it. Oh—here it comes! An impact only we'd sense. But it's neither its death nor the end. Five . . ."

D kept walking. Not pausing for even a second, he began to descend the staircase.

"Four . . ."

In the midst of the darkness, the giant heaved a long sigh.

"Three . . ."

In one tiny village in a western Frontier sector, a family of three awoke.

"Two . . ."

D halted. He was in the middle of the staircase.

"One . . ."

The star was swallowed by a land of great forests and tundra.

"Zero."

It was quiet. A silence gripped the world as if time itself had stopped.

Then, when the hoarse voice finally told him, "There it goes," the gorgeous young man in black who'd been like a sculpture of death finally began walking again.

"Half a northern Frontier sector was laid to waste!" the hoarse voice continued.

The Hunter's eyes as well might have beheld that vision of death.

II

It was two days later that the survey party from the Northern Frontier Administration Bureau set out for the area where the meteorite had landed.

"This is just . . ." The young geologist was going to say *horrible*, but the spectacle before his eyes had finally robbed him of his speech.

It was a sight that no one could ignore. The roar that assailed their ears was that of a muddy torrent that snaked by in a thick ocher flow just a few yards from where the men had frozen on their mounts. And there wasn't just muddy water. Titanic trees floated by, the places where they'd snapped in two showing plain as day— and the dull thuds that rang out from time to time were the sound of these countless boles banging into one another. As if tethered to the trees, the remains of enormous armored beasts and other unidentifiable monsters also flowed past—as did human corpses.

"The ice on the tundra's melted."

"It'll still take two days to reach where it came down. And yet here we are, running into a river like this? The damn thing's gotta be dozens of yards across!"

Another of them pulled out a map and a photo and compared them to the scene before them. The river was easily in excess of five hundred yards wide, and while the spray from the water didn't create it, a fog hung over the opposite shore that kept them from making out anything on that side. There wasn't any trace of the great stands of trees depicted on their map. For that matter, it didn't show this river, either.

"There's bound to be more of this. I say screw it!"

"Shut up, Dan. Back in the Capital, folks are sitting on pins and needles waiting for word from us, you know. I don't care if it's a river or the sea; if it's in our way, we're crossing it. Start getting ready for a fording right away."

Nearly twenty men dismounted in unison and began to take their gear down off their horses' backs.

"We're all set with the ropes!" someone shouted twenty or thirty minutes later, and another twenty minutes after that, explosions rang out overhead.

Rocket launchers shot ropes to the unseen opposite shore, and special metal-alloy drill tips on the ends of the ropes bored down dozens of yards into the earth to secure them. When the current was strong, there was no other way to cross with their horses except to hold onto these ropes.

Resigned to their pitiful lot, the group members looked up to the sky as one.

"What in the world's that?"

"Choppers, I think."

"Whose?"

These shouted remarks were in response to five aircraft flying purposefully across the cloudy, ash gray sky.

"I don't think any of the villages around here own anything like that—which can only mean . . ."

The rest of that sentence had already formed in the heart of every man present.

"They're bandits!"

"Those bastards—they're fucking ghouls! They'll loot the place dry!" another man cursed, the words rising with the sound of his teeth grinding.

But this became a cry of astonishment when all five helicopters were thrown off course simultaneously and dropped behind that silky veil that wasn't quite spray or mist. Rotor struck rotor, throwing free chunks that impacted on still other aircraft—and no sooner had this happened than the sky was filled with fiery lotus blossoms. Black smoke spread in the air and flames consumed hundreds of pieces of debris as all the crimson blooms scattered their petals. Once they'd vanished into the depths of the fog, only the smoke snaked into the sky, and then that too disappeared.

"What the hell happened?"

"Turbulence?"

"The wind ain't blowing all that hard—the meteorite's gotta be to blame. A cursed star is what it is!"

"Damn! If we get too close, we're liable to drown. We'd do well to turn back, boss."

"Shut your pie hole. Josh, you're gonna be the first to go across."

"Shit. I wish I'd kept quiet."

Ultimately it took half the day for the whole group to cross the stream, dodging oncoming trees and corpses floating in the current. Not only was it more than five hundred yards wide, but they also had to get their horses and baggage across, too. The dense fog hid any scenery more than three feet away behind endless white, so the leader ordered the men to form a circle and to be sure to keep tabs on the people to either side of them.

"The ground's mush."

"Yeah. And it's warm."

"You think maybe there was a volcano or something in the area?"

"Nope. That wasn't it. It's still warm on account of the friction when the meteorite struck."

"You've gotta be kidding me! That was two days ago. This should've long since cooled."

"Which tells us something—the meteorite itself is still boiling hot. Just look. We're still two days' journey from where it fell, yet every last tree's been uprooted. The ice hereabouts runs a foot thick, but it's been turned into this river and the fog. Every village we've passed up till now was knocked flat by a quake or swallowed by cracks in the earth. Hills crumbled, swamps boiled away, and there's not a bird or a beast to be seen. I don't care how big a meteorite we're talking about; there's no way it could do all this. On top of that, the communiqué from the Capital said astronomers watching the shooting star reported that it was just a little deal, less than eight inches in diameter. There's no way in hell it could've caused a disaster of this proportion."

"Why didn't you say anything about that before, boss?" a number of them asked.

Their leader replied impassively, "Oh, that's simple. Because if I'd let that slip, there's not a man among you who would've come along!"

"Well, you're right about that, but still—"

Just then, the old huntsman who'd been by the campfire with his eyes shut tight put his finger to his lips and shushed them.

"What is it, Pops?" the leader asked.

"Something's coming from the north. And it's headed this way at a hell of a speed," he said.

"What is it?"

"I don't know. Hey, put that fire out. Everyone, don't make a sound, now."

The whole group grew tense. Aside from the old huntsman, they were all farmers who'd just signed on for the per diem and the reputation that came from having taken part in a survey party. But farmers were only used to dealing with the sort of supernatural creatures and monsters that ravaged their fields. Scattering an extinguishing powder on their campfire, they grabbed their respective weapons and took cover behind their baggage—all without a single extraneous action.

A minute passed. After another thirty seconds had gone by, red points of light appeared in the depths of the fog.

"Here they come," the old huntsman said, cocking the old-fashioned rifle he carried.

The points of light swiftly grew from the size of a fingertip to that of a fist, and by this time the outline of the things had become visible as black silhouettes in the fog. From the bottom of cylinders about six and a half feet tall, a number of thin pipes wriggled like tentacles. A red point of light glowed from a spot about halfway up each cylinder. There were more than a dozen of these things.

The leader looked at the huntsman. When it came to combat, he was a veteran.

The old huntsman ignored him. His instincts had been triggered by the approaching foe. The same instincts that time and again had pulled him back from the jaws of death into the land of the living told him not to mess with this. They weren't telling him to run—just not to mess with it.

But before the huntsman could take any action, hostilities were declared.

"Draw them in before you open fire," the leader ordered his group.

The silhouettes glided closer. They'd heard him.

"Fire!"

The shout was followed by ear-shattering reports, while the old huntsman leaned his rifle up against his pack and grabbed the right lapel of his fire-beast vest. Telling himself to calm down, the old man focused his attention on his own fingertip, which soon found something hard and thin.

Up ahead, screams split the night air. A tentacle had just snared one member of the party. Legs thrashing, he was hoisted up into the air. Along the way, he raised his rifle and fired. There was the sound of something hard being struck, and his slug changed direction.

The cylinders were now plainly visible. Entirely silver, they were supported by two of the tentacles, which seemed to be tied to them by iron rings. The other six tentacles were apparently meant for combat, and they seized another member of the party who'd taken cover under his baggage by the ankle and effortlessly pulled him out again.

Screams rang out here and there. The crack of rifles followed, and soon there was silence.

The men hadn't abandoned resistance voluntarily. As they were struggling in midair, a tentacle had been put against the back of each man's head, and from the end of it a slim needle had penetrated the skull. Although it didn't look as if the needles had pierced very deeply, this attack had a horrifying effect on the party members. There was a slight pain in their heads—as if something were flowing out from them to nowhere in particular. And that was the last thing the men felt before they lost consciousness—and their lives. By the time their limp bodies were thrown to the ground, they'd already stopped breathing.

Scanning wildly all the while, the cylinders passed over the dead, and then they finally spotted the old huntsman crouched down behind his baggage. A tentacle stretched from one of the approaching cylinders and touched the base of his neck. It soon came away again, and as if they'd lost all interest, the cylinders disappeared without another moment's hesitation into the mist from which they'd come—into the depths of the steam.

After the tentacles that could be called sensors had registered whether the person they came into contact with was living or dead, a long, needlelike suction device drew out what was essentially the core of his life force. A human's life force flowed through his body from the chakra. As a human reached higher mental and physical levels, the chakra shifted to a loftier position, with the chakra in the back of the head linking human beings to the power of the universe. This is why when people had ascended to an existence that was more than human, they'd been depicted in ancient artwork as saints with glowing halos behind their heads. Undoubtedly that was the reason the cylinders chose to extract the life force from the back of the head.

The shore lay under the stillness of death. While the sound of the river hadn't died out, it still felt that way. This was probably due to the blanket of pitiful corpses. When an hour had passed since the butchers had left, there was movement in this dead world. It came at the moment when dawn tinged the eastern sky blue, its light spreading across the cruel ground like faint wings. It was the corpse of the old huntsman. His body had been like a mummy's, with its pulse stopped, brain waves gone, and every trace of life missing, but now it was returning to life. The blood pumped fiercely through his body, his heart beat strongly, and he opened his eyes. Then, closing his eyes for a few seconds to reflect back on what'd happened an hour ago, he strangely enough reached for the very same spot on the back of his head where the cylinders had drained the life from his compatriots and pulled out a long, thin needle. A foot in length, the needle was stark white beast bone—and he'd learned where to jab it from his father, who in turn had learned the trick from his grandfather.

If you're in the forest or out on the tundra and can't move, and you don't think you've got enough food to last till help comes, press here. When you do, you'll become a corpse. Aside from the very smallest of arteries, which will carry blood to your brain to keep it from dying, you'll be a dead body in all other respects. And no one will be able to detect that pulse. Depending on how you push the needle in, you can make it last a half hour or an hour, a year, or even a decade if you like.

His father had told him he'd survive all that time without anything to eat or drink, and that he had to make sure there were no wild beasts around before using the needle on the appropriate spot.

Your grandfather's grandfather said that a long, long time ago, these things with bodies like cylinders and snaking tentacles appeared and started killing folks like crazy. Our ancestor was the only one to survive because at the time he happened to be doing these experiments with needles.

The old huntsman mouthed something softly: words of thanks to his father and his ancestors.

Looking out across the gruesome tableau, he muttered, "I'm gonna have to get these boys buried."

And with that he reached for the rifle leaning up against his pack. Once it was back in his hands, he was transformed into a professional on the hunt. By the time the stock came to rest against his shoulder, he already had the hammer cocked. The two-pound rifle meant for killing armored fire dragons was trained unwaveringly on the muddy flow; the huntsman's ears had detected a change in the water's roar.

III

The old huntsman's eye caught an arm reaching for shore from the muddy torrent. Appearing to struggle against being washed downstream, a second arm appeared, and a moment later the whole body popped up. While it couldn't exactly be described as effortless, the figure managed to collapse on land after being pushed just a foot or two further by the water.

The old huntsman called out to the wheezing form, "That you, boss?"

The mud-covered figure jumped up, but his tension passed as soon as he saw the old man.

"Pops!" he said, letting out a deep breath. "I'm glad you made it. The fact that those damned things didn't go into the water saved my skin. I suppose everyone else . . ."

The old huntsman nodded. "They all bought it. You're lucky to be alive—oh, but you're a veteran fish trapper, aren't you?"

Though the leader tried to smile, he couldn't.

For generations, his family had made a living hunting the fish that lived in the ponds and lakes near his village. Up to ten feet long, these fish were voracious carnivores, but there wasn't one of them that the leader's family couldn't land with ease. The leader was better than anyone at this sort of hunting because of the way he'd been raised—he could stop his breathing and remain underwater for more than an hour.

"When they grabbed Roscoe, I jumped into the water. I clung to some weeds—damn, I must've been scared, because I couldn't come out for over an hour. Anyway, I'm glad you survived, too. From here on out, having someone else along should be more reassuring than going it alone."

"You don't mean to tell me you intend to keep going?" the old huntsman said, his eyes growing wide. "Those things will be up ahead. Probably worse stuff, too."

As he got his breathing under control, the leader lay flat on his back on the ground again.

"I can't help it. See, that's the job. Back in the village, everyone's scared stiff, waiting for our return. I can't very well be the only one to come moping back. For starters, it'd mean all the rest of these guys died for nothing."

At this point, he finally realized something.

"Oh, I can't force you to go along with me, Pops. You're lucky to have survived. You don't just turn around and throw all that away. I'll continue on alone from here on out—Godspeed to you."

"At any rate, let's get everyone buried," the old man said, gazing at where light hung in the eastern sky. "Then we'll set out. Get as far inland as we can while we've got daylight. I'll go along with you."

After burying eight corpses and taking a short rest, they ended up embarking just past noon. Before they'd walked an hour, the pair found their surroundings had begun to take on a weirder aspect. With the gradual thinning of the fog they could see quite far into the distance, but all that greeted their eyes was a wasteland. Perhaps it would've been better to call it desolation. Black soil spread as far as the eye could see. There was no sign of any living creatures, and the pair was surrounded by such a vast expanse that the glowing red lights of those cylindrical things would've almost been a welcome sight. With provisions and weapons on their backs, the two men sank ankle deep into the miry ground, and steam hid the blue vault of the heavens, although it also occasionally filled the pair's field of view with rainbows, as if to atone for its sins.

Two hours passed, and then two became four. Just as they were about to enter their fifth hour, there was a change in their environment. The boots they pulled up out of the mud met the one thing the pair presently desired more than anything—solid ground.

"Huh?"

After glancing down at their feet, the pair looked across the earth stretching into the distance. It could've been described as a silvery land.

"What the hell is this?" the leader asked, sounding unnerved.

Here was a man who'd been chosen to lead a survey party in exploring the unknown, and he burned with such a sense of duty he still pressed forward even after watching most of his men get killed. He certainly wasn't a coward. But his voice was quaking.

"Damned if I know," the huntsman said, shaking his head. "I don't know what it is, but it's sure as hell gonna be like this all the way to where that meteorite fell. We've gone and stepped into a whole other world."

"What kind of *other world* are we talking about here?"

"Good question."

"You mean like the world of the Nobility?"

"Probably."

Something about the huntsman's tone bothered the leader.

"Is it or isn't it? Spell it out for me, man!"

"It's just a hunch."

"Oh."

Halting, the old huntsman adjusted the pack strapped to his back. He soon started walking again.

"Nobles are Nobles—but this is some different kind of Noble, or so I think," the old man said.

"Different? You mean to tell me there are other kinds of Nobility?"

"I don't know. That's why I said it's just a hunch."

"Well, I trust your hunch," the leader said, looking all around with a chilled expression.

There was only fog and silvery terrain. No hills, no trees, no tundra locked away under eternal ice. Even after twilight fell, the pair continued walking in the darkness. They were afraid to stop. From time to time the leader pulled out his map and survey records and checked their position, but he did so while they were still on the move. The further they advanced, the more a terror and despair that had nothing to do with their exhaustion spread through their hearts, now heavy and dark.

We'll never make it back. We're gonna die out here.

Despite this, however, both pairs of eyes gleamed with a resolute determination to fight. Even if they were going to die, they had to see what lay out there. And without fail, they'd get word of what they discovered to those who waited.

In the middle of the night, they took a rest. The leader had collapsed. When he awoke, it was past noon. The fog and the featureless silver land stretched on forever. For quite some time, both men had held in their hearts a certain conviction: *This land is man made.* But who could've made something so incredible? Who'd packed it away in an eight-inch meteorite?

After having something to eat, they started walking again. And the old huntsman ended up telling a story about a giant he'd seen in the western Frontier sectors when he was young.

"You know, Pops, you're a good-enough shot to hit an angel worm from a mile away. You've got nerve enough to take on a Sanki dragon with no more than a machete, so no one can fault you there. You shouldn't be rotting away on some lousy little mountain bagging birds and beasts to sell their meat when you could go to the Capital and find a better job. So, why don't you?" the leader asked, and that's how the tale got started.

"It was quite a ways back," the old man said, starting the story.

Like so many other young men with boundless confidence in their own strength, he'd wandered through various parts of the Frontier looking for an opportunity to make a name for himself. At the time, he heard about a legendary creature that would eat every beast off a mountain in a year's time, then move onto the next mountain to sate its appetite, and that sparked a desire for honor and combat that burned like a flame in the young huntsman. When he headed up the same kind of mountain where he lived even now with no more than his trusty rifle, it wasn't out of rashness at all. Rather, it was merely a manifestation of his youthful fervor. For a whole month he moved among the colossal boles and weirdly shaped rock as if he were the lord of the mountain, but he'd abandoned the search and was on his way back down when he was swallowed by a thick fog. As soon as he decided to bivouac there, the fog grew even denser, and it showed no sign of clearing any time soon. Not even the wind blew.

On his third night camping out there, the situation suddenly took a stranger turn. From the swirling white depths of the fog, a gigantic figure appeared, accompanied by a great rumbling in the earth.

"When I was a wee young'un, I'd seen the same thing in a picture book all about the Nobility. It was a giant beast that combined machinery with an artificial life form. More than a dozen feet high it stood, wearing rusty old armor and a helm and carrying an iron club with its hairy arms. As for its face, I suppose you could say it looked like a crazy person. Its eyes were vacant, and drool ran down from the corner of its mouth like a waterfall. Black drool, at that. Even now I can still recall how it reeked of oil. There was just one thing that bothered me then, and still bothers me now. According to that picture book, that type of creature had supposedly been dubbed a failure, and they were freed from computer control and destroyed by the Nobility more than five thousand years ago."

The beast had headed straight toward the huntsman. Pure luck was the only way to describe the way the man managed to dodge the iron club the thing swung down at him—but the way he got off a shot with his rifle as he was rolling around on the ground was the work of a born huntsman. His bullet hit the giant beast right in the middle of the face, and the creature's upper body jerked back.

"Well, I thought I'd hit it dead bang. And that was the way it looked, too. But the thing didn't fall. It didn't even drop to one knee; it just spat up a wad of blood, which landed at my feet. But what I'd thought was a wad of blood turned out to be a bloodstained slug and one of that thing's fangs. Why, that freak—"

Seven hundred and fifty miles per hour—his bullet had flown nearly at the speed of sound, and the thing had stopped it with its fangs, giving a whole new meaning to the expression "biting the bullet."

The huntsman was so stunned that he didn't get another shot off until the creature charged him. Made in desperation, his second shot hit its chest protector and ricocheted off, while his third streaked through empty space, for the giant had unexpectedly leapt to one side.

In the fog to his right there was a great forest. From it echoed the sounds of enormous trees being snapped or uprooted by something that was approaching with tremendous speed. The giant beast only had time to loose a single howl of insanity. Because what bounded from the fog was a figure every bit as titanic as itself.

"His coat and cape were in tatters—but I could tell at a glance they'd both been crafted from the finest materials. I swear, I'll never understand why Nobles would ever use anything as flimsy as all that when they could've made the same thing from indestructible metal fibers."

The giant's weapon was a long spear. Carved with intricate designs, it was well over fifteen feet long, and the keenness of the point that ran almost half its length was just as imposing as his foe's iron club.

The giant beast struck first. Though the Nobility had created this creature for combat, those same Nobles had decided that the control DNA in this type alone hadn't functioned properly. The iron club it brought down appeared just as fast as the huntsman's bullets. But it rebounded, and then the giant beast, leaning forward from the attack, was knocked away. As it lurched, a gleam of light streaked at its neck.

After deflecting the club with its shaft, the long spear had spun around to cut through the opponent's neck, and then, in the giant's black-gloved hands, it spun in another great arc before halting.

"I watched the whole thing there from behind a tree, out of sight. Right off the bat, I knew it had to be a giant straight out of the legends. Dangling from the shoulders of that red cape of his were the corpses of greater elk and twin-headed bears. Maybe he didn't notice me—more likely he did and just wasn't worried about me. Toting the body of the giant beast like it was nothing, he headed back into the same fog he came from. I didn't go after him. Hell, I was scared. It had to be a Noble. But what kind of Noble can walk around free as you please in the light of the sun? The mere thought of what he really was makes my hair stand on end."

And yet, about five minutes after the sound of the giant's footfalls had faded completely, he chambered a new round in his rifle and went after the enormous figure. And then, high above the ground where the giant's footprints remained so clearly, he saw an enormous head glaring down at him. The instant he realized it was the severed head of the giant beast, he turned around without a word and climbed down the mountain that very day.

ABOUT THE AUTHOR

Hideyuki Kikuchi was born in Chiba, Japan, in 1949. He attended the prestigious Aoyama University and wrote his first novel, *Demon City Shinjuku*, in 1982. Over the past two decades, Kikuchi has written numerous horror novels, and is one of Japan's leading horror masters, working in the tradition of occidental horror writers like Fritz Leiber, Robert Bloch, H. P. Lovecraft, and Stephen King. As of 2004, there were seventeen novels in his hugely popular ongoing Vampire Hunter D series. Many live-action and anime movies of the 1980s and 1990s have been based on Kikuchi's novels.

ABOUT THE ILLUSTRATOR

Yoshitaka Amano was born in Shizuoka, Japan. He is well known as a manga and anime artist, and is the famed designer for the *Final Fantasy* game series. Amano took part in designing characters for many of Tatsunoko Productions' greatest cartoons, including *Gatchaman* (released in the U.S. as *G-Force* and *Battle of the Planets*). Amano became a freelancer at the age of thirty and has collaborated with numerous writers, creating nearly twenty illustrated books that have sold millions of copies. Since the late 1990s, Amano has worked with several American comics publishers, including DC Comics on the illustrated Sandman novel *Sandman: The Dream Hunters* with Neil Gaiman, and Marvel Comics on *Elektra and Wolverine: The Redeemer* with best-selling author Greg Rucka.